SNOW WHITE

Bernhard Kammel born in 1962, is the grandson of a distinguished Bohemian architect Leo Kammel, stemming from a family of established glass industrialists and glass artists. Between 1980 and 1995 Bernhard studied architecture, theology and forestry in Vienna.

While attending high school he published short stories and feature articles in leading newspapers and continued to write plays, lyrics and essays later on in life. He also produced fine art photography, and since 1999, large-format narrative tableaux.

In 2005, he founded his film production company and has since made several films, which have been invited to compete at major festivals, garnering a number of awards. In 2018, he founded REAKTOR, a transdisciplinary art establishment in Vienna, the programming of which is orientated towards contemporary cultural events. Bernhard lives in a secluded location in the foothills of the Alps and breeds Lipizzans.

SNOW WHITE

A NOVELLA

Bernhard Kammel

Translated by
Stephen Grynwasser

Om Books International

First published in 2023 by

Om Books International

Corporate & Editorial Office
A-12, Sector 64, Noida 201 301
Uttar Pradesh, India
Phone: +91 120 477 4100
Email: editorial@ombooks.com
Website: www.ombooksinternational.com

Sales Office
107, Ansari Road, Darya Ganj,
New Delhi 110 002, India
Phone: +91 11 4000 9000
Email: sales@ombooks.com
Website: www.ombooks.com

ISBN: 978-93-94046-04-7

Printed in India

10 9 8 7 6 5 4 3 2 1

FOR FRANZI

I

More drained emotionally than physically exhausted, Atam sat down on one of the very objects he found so repulsive. Indeed, he could feel, through the seat of his trousers, the hideous pattern of the fabric upholstery covering the seats of the bus. He could feel the coarse hand of that barbaric mix of cheap synthetic threads and discarded pure wool. Already, he wanted to leap up and shake out his clothing, as if that might *ex tunc* eliminate the contact – knowing fully well it was impossible. And so, his thighs and back remained tightly coiled, ready to spring; yet his stomach and toes failed to follow suit, and so, half-crouched, he remained where he was.

Everything seemed to fit, match and suit, as if grotesque processes always proceeded reasonably in reality, as if the disturbing and the hostile had the most solid of structures and an axiomatic premise, from which everything flowed consequentially.

It had all begun when he woke up next to Gretchen, who had hardly slept a wink, crying all night as she leant against Atam on the sofa in her sports attire, sticky with sweat, flushing all her mascara onto Atam's shirt collar. She had left

Atam no time to change or to have breakfast. Not even a cup of coffee had been allowed, Gretchen threw him out as soon as it was daybreak.

Under the sway of the stop-and-go motion of the bus, his head fell forward onto his chest, then all the way back again. The diesel engine droned on and on as the drive shaft rubbed against the floor plate, causing the entire body of the passenger compartment to vibrate. As he wiped his forehead, he noticed his frayed shirt cuff with the missing button. He recalled the moment he had lost that button and pushed aside the *now* to contemplate the hours ahead with an attentiveness and alertness that made it seem as if yesterday had never existed. He had become quite curious and closed his eyes, which, only a moment ago, had scrutinised his new surroundings so defensively, and felt his head surrender to the swaying motion until the moment the vehicle pulled into its terminus at Schottenring and Atam alighted.

Opposite his stop, he stared at the large and imposing administrative building of what had once been the Creditanstalt-Bankverein. On this side, it was closed off to customer traffic due to construction work, as the bright letters on the large information hoardings informed him.

The windows on the ground floor were all boarded up. Skips filled with building rubble were now parked where limousines had once lined the pavement in an absolute no-stopping zone. A cloud of dust billowed continually out of the studded main entrance portal, its shimmering colours changing minute by minute from beige to orangey-purple. From inside the building, he could hear a continual droning and pounding that caused the entire street to tremble.

Atam entered through the main entrance and stepped through the haze of dust, into the bowels of the building. In the large cashiers' hall beyond the foyer, a fountain rose in the centre, bursting through the blanket of dust into the atrium above. The floor was completely covered in a fine powder, obscuring any sight of the stone slabs beneath. This thick layer of powder muffled his footsteps and sustained the vortices he left behind with each footfall. He circumnavigated the centre of the room with its gyrating vortex of dust and reached the wall at the far end, opposite the main entrance. On a whim he opted to turn westwards, in the general direction of St. Stephen's Cathedral.

The swing doors were unlocked and moved without creaking. Offering no resistance, they opened easily as Atam pushed against them and, once he had stepped through onto an unexpectedly clean floor, they swung back casually, drawn by springs fatigued by many years of loyal service. He was now standing in the adjacent foyer, the one that could be accessed from Schottenbastei through a side entrance that was still open. A sign hanging from the high ceiling on long delicate chains dangled in the draught, pointing the way down to the makeshift room on the basement floor that contained the safe deposit boxes.

He descended a sweeping staircase of beige marble only to find himself in front of a wide row of glass doors blocking off the whole of the deserted corridor; none of the doors could be pushed open. Spreading out beyond the doors was a large yet low-ceilinged hall into which sturdy metal lockers had been arranged that ran the length of the walls, as temporary safe deposit boxes. The entire hall was lit from above by an illuminated ceiling similar to the one in the main cashiers' hall. As there was no place for anyone to hide, Atam instantly caught sight of Harmstedter, Gretchen's divorced husband.

Harmstedter must have sensed his presence; in any case, he suddenly turned towards him and set eyes on him. With a contemptuous look, he motioned for him to enter. Atam rattled several of the swing doors, but none gave way or opened. Harmstedter uttered a shrill, malicious laugh. Through the glass panels, Atam could hear him sneering that he may have managed to seduce his wife, but he was clearly incapable of stepping through a doorway in a civilised manner.

Atam shrugged his shoulders questioningly. Then he began to shake his head and stare at Harmstedter as the latter pulled a handgun complete with silencer from the plastic bag he was carrying, angrily signalling Atam off to the side. What happened next occurred both in a flash and in slow motion. Atam perceived, in real time, the crashing sound of shattering glass and, out of time, watched the shards of glass fly through the room as if frozen in their trajectories. Harmstedter collapsed, his head striking an intact pane of glass, his fleshy cheek squashed up against it as he slid downwards before striking the full-length marble floor.

Atam stepped through the impacted swing door and turned Harmstedter over onto his back to see if he was still alive; but somehow Harmstedter had managed to shoot himself dead, a victim of his own ricochet. A frayed gash ran across his forehead, brain oozing from it, shimmering from beige to orangey purple and foaming with faintly pulsating brain fluid. The alarm went off. 'He who lives by the sword shall perish by the sword' was the thought that occurred to Atam as he eased the plastic bag from the grip of Harmstedter's still supple fingers. Inside the bag, Atam found a pack of photographs, which he quickly took out. A cursory glance at the photos on the top told him that these were baryta prints depicting trees in the Burggarten, and he wondered why Gretchen thought they might in some way be compromising.

But he had no time to investigate the matter further if he was to make a swift exit and avoid any awkward questioning by the police; in any case, he was keen to spare Gretchen any further trouble. There was no evidence of any video surveillance cameras in the room with the safe deposit boxes, which had once been a WC area. He hurriedly restored Harmstedter to the position he had last assumed of his own dying accord and stepped back through the shattered glass door into the corridor without closing Harmstedter's eyes, something for which he felt remorse but was out of the question on account of forensics.

No sooner had he climbed the stairs back up to the ground floor than he turned, without pausing, into the vast expanse of the cashiers' hall. None of his tracks was visible, and yet, behind the roller of billowing dust that was now tending towards an orangey hue, he spotted a squad of police officers fanning out from the main entrance, combing through the cashiers' hall at some pace, as if to cut off his escape route. Atam immediately directed his footsteps opposite towards the dark corridor.

II

The policemen did not appear to have spotted his trail; at least, they did not enter his own corridor. He was hurrying down the corridor towards the staircase at the rear when he became aware of footsteps in high heels approaching from the other end: staccato steps evidently reined in by a tight-fitting skirt. He was trying to catch a glimpse of the woman as she approached in the dim light of the corridor against the bright glare reflected off the chalk-white walls from the stairway into the ground floor when suddenly he sneezed.

The footsteps stopped instantly. But she did not turn back. She remained where she was, peering into the corridor. He raised his hand and beckoned her over. She resumed her stride and came closer, though in a much slower pace than when she had first spotted him. He greeted the woman in the grey suit with a nod of the head and a slight bow.

Briefly, she raised her right hand, gloved in white leather. He set out to kiss it and introduce himself but could utter no sound; rather, he began to cough and cough some more. The woman in the grey suit took the thermos flask out of her clutch bag, opened it and poured hot steaming coffee into the unscrewed cup. Atam sipped hastily at first, then emptied the rest in one long draught and handed the cup back to her. While questioning through her eyes alone, she poured out some more coffee. And without thinking, he defensively placed his hand over the cup. As the hot coffee struck the back of his hand, he was about to say something, but delicately, she put her gloved index finger to her lips and closed her eyes for an instant.

It was a gesture his mother had always used conspiratorially whenever she wanted her young son to be quiet after she had put him to bed and did not want to hear any more of his stories which could likely get him all excited again; it was, after all, bedtime. He cheerfully followed the attractive, unknown woman like his admired mother back then, and said nothing. His stomach rumbled softly. She heard it, glanced up almost guiltily, then carefully checked each door in the corridor. Then, she took him by the hand and pulled him along from door to door until they entered an empty staff room-cum-kitchenette.

There was a small window opposite the door, with barely any light penetrating its dirty grey glass. There was the smell of dust along with detergent and even a hint of mould. They both began to open drawers and push them shut again like a new parlour game of some kind. Atam came across the fridge, stimulated by the sound, opened its door. A pack of congealed milk was stuck to a glass shelf. The butter compartment contained some sort of medicine.

Suddenly, the woman let out a yelp. Up on the top shelf, she had found a coffee-brown cardboard box with a colourful printed design on it. Centuryfood, it said, in large orangey-red letters. 'Help me,' she chuckled in a high pitched voice, wiggling her behind teasingly in her attempt to reach out; Atam's first impulse was in fact to grab her by the waist and lift her up. She stepped aside and, furrowing her brow, pointed upwards. Atam took out the box and placed it on the countertop in front of her. She ripped the box open along the perforation, flipped the thin cardboard lid aside and uncovered a multitude of chocolate bars individually wrapped in plastic film. Atam felt he too had to contribute something. He kneeled down to check the space under the kitchen sink and found an assortment of household cleaning agents. Behind them, he spotted a jute bag.

He reached inside and, with his fingers, felt a selection of nuts and sultanas. Affixed to it was a label shaped like a bishop's mitre. The woman gave him an admiring look and took charge of the bag. She looked around for chairs so they could sit down. Since there was no seating arrangement anywhere in the kitchen, they stepped back out into the corridor but still could not find a comfortable spot to settle down behind any of the doors nearby.

Somehow, they had managed to make their way back to the cashiers' hall when they saw a cohort of policemen striding rapidly towards the swing doors. 'Oh God, they're after me!' shouted Atam. He turned around suddenly and, grabbing the woman by the hand, ran down the corridor as fast as her skirt would allow, back towards the stairwell. He directed their steps down into the basement. The woman shrieked excitedly and followed him blindly.

They passed a series of doors numbered consecutively, then reached a door marked 'OBSERVATORY'. As they entered, a gentle draught wafted towards them, wrenching the door handle from Atam's grip as it clunked firmly into the lock behind them.

He felt around for a light switch. There was none. But daylight was shining in through the glass tiles on the ceiling at the other end of the room and, as their eyes adjusted to the darkness, it bathed everything in a gentle pale blue-grey that matched most fetchingly the woman's grey suit, her dark eyes and her blue-grey eye shadow.

The woman's eyes were open wide, with her heart beating rapidly. He could sense the scent of her lipstick and deodorant as well as her excitement. Atam took off his jacket, shook it out and laid it at her feet. He motioned her to sit down on it. She accepted Atam's invitation, even though it made little-to-no sense to picnic on the out-of-date chocolate bars in a basement while on the run.

Gracefully, she slid to the floor, folded her legs outwards from under her bottom and settled down, leaning slightly forward at the waist. Atam looked at her calves in the dim light as they softly curved away from her skirt. Around her ankle he noticed a delicate silver chain underneath her dark blue stockings.

'I haven't had a chance to introduce myself,' Atam began. The woman giggled bashfully. He crouched down in front of her and took her hand, feigning to kiss the back of it. 'I'm Andrea,' she replied, holding out her hand. 'And why exactly are we running from the police?' Atam replied that he wasn't sure but didn't want to risk finding out. He had found a body down by the safe deposit boxes and did not want to become unnecessarily implicated in the case. 'Oh my goodness, how exciting,' commented Andrea.

They huddled on the basement floor for quite a while in the semi-darkness illuminated by the broken glass ceiling behind them as Andrea fed him. They took turns biting into the chocolate. She could be heard swallowing first, then he. They took turns looking into each other's eyes and by the time they had finished off their supplies, they stared at each other for the first time and his stomach began rumbling again. 'We need to do something about that stomach of yours,' Andrea said, getting up and pulling him even further back towards the glass ceiling.

Street noise crept in through the glass tile ceiling, half of which was sunken in. Clearly, they were already well beyond the confines of the building. A cold wind swept in through the hole in the ceiling, causing Andrea's hair to flutter against her cheeks. Atam took the handbag from Andrea's hands and stuffed the photographs into it. He then interlaced the fingers of both hands to form a stirrup and held them out invitingly in front of Andrea's knee. She stepped into the stirrup and pulled herself up by the back of his neck with both hands, then swung herself up onto the pavement, sat down on the edge of the hole in the ceiling and let her legs dangle down encouragingly.

'Come on up,' she said to Atam teasingly, who then tossed her handbag up to her and jumped up after it. They sat next to each other on the pavement on Atam's jacket and Andrea opened her handbag. 'May I?' she asked, pulling out the photos. 'These are wonderful photos,' Andrea said, 'really professional. Are you a photographer?' Atam shook his head: 'It's because of them that I was down at the safe deposit boxes. I was supposed to pick them up from the person who took them and bring them back to her.' 'We'll take them to her together,' Andrea replied, and as they stood up, she added, 'We'll do everything together from now on.'

Hand in hand, they walked alongside the building they had just escaped from, then crossed the street. As they got further away from it, the former bank headquarters of the Creditanstalt looked gloomier. Dark grey only in those areas where rainwater had washed away the dust, otherwise black. Its windows blinded by dust reflected a grey-filtered sky. Against such a backdrop, the passing cars and construction workers looked positively colourful and bright. Even the policemen – now emerging from a side corridor – livened up the urban landscape with their uniforms and yellow wellingtons.

Atam spotted them before they could notice him. Pulling Andrea down behind him, the two of them squatted among the parked cars. Their knees touched. Their eyes met. Andrea found herself unable to suppress a giggle. Her infectious happiness prompted him to laugh even louder until they were both helpless with squeals of laughter, barely able to maintain their crouched position. Finally, now carefree and with all the day's bad events laughed away, they eventually stood up. Atam glanced back towards the side exit once more and saw the policemen looking over towards them. But they were not showing any interest in Atam and Andrea, nor did they seem to have any intention of making their way across to where the two of them were now standing.

III

Andrea led the way, taking him by the hand. She began to skip like a little girl, seemingly propelled by the sheer exuberance of their laughter as she trotted along. She achieved quite a pace in this manner, and it took some effort on Atam's part to keep up with her as he tagged along behind.

They spotted a sausage stand on the other side of the Ringstrasse. It was made of dark brown anodised aluminium, with large expanses of glass all around, as if to showcase the sausage lady herself. But she was in fact almost hidden by the large pickle jars that acted like magnifying glasses whenever she stood directly behind them. The sliding window itself was slightly ajar, with various patrons threaded around the narrow buffet ledge. A sweet, pungent odour wafted over them.

Andrea watched the sausage lady impatiently, who did not appear to be making any move to put fresh sausages into the pan. 'Are those fresh ones?' she asked. 'All my sausages are fresh, Madam,' the sausage lady replied. Andrea felt needled and retorted, 'I can tell with just a single bite, you know!' The sausage lady quickly threw a fresh pair of sausages into the boiling water which hissed and spat, raising the question of whether this was in fact a tacit admission that the sausages already floating in the pan were being reheated after all. The matter was instantly settled when a new customer just pulled up.

'Busy today,' remarked the newcomer to the sausage lady from behind Atam and Andrea. 'Always, *Herr Kommerzialrat*,' she replied, flashing her teeth. 'Can you shift over to the side a bit, so I can serve *Herr Kommerzialrat*?' This was Atam's cue: 'Well, if you hand over our order, we'll be only too happy to move aside. After all, we were here first.' 'Of course,' the sausage woman replied with a conciliatory shrug of her shoulders. She fished around the sausage pan, pulled out two pairs of sausages and placed them on high-sided oblong porcelain plates. She slathered goulash sauce over the sausages, and then asked, 'Slice of bread or bread roll?'

Atam and Andrea retreated around the corner. Shielded by the aluminium body of the sausage stand, which kept the other patrons and the dust-laden wind at bay, Andrea cut the sausages into bite-sized pieces on both plates. Atam's stomach began to rumble once again, but she had already begun to feed him the first piece of sausage that she dragged through the sauce on his plate. She monitored his progress carefully while she herself chewed hurriedly.

Andrea then broke open a bread roll and dipped it deep into the sauce on her plate. She let the excess sauce drain off, shook off large drops of it with gentle and controlled movements of her fragrant wrist before placing the piece in Atam's mouth.

She then pushed one glass towards Atam and let her fingers linger on the glass longer than was strictly necessary. As he put his fingers over hers, almost shyly she withdrew her fingers from his grasp but not without soothingly brushing the back of his hand with the fingertips of both her ring and little finger.

With great relish, he downed a mouthful of beer in one draught. Whitish foam stuck to his upper lip. Andrea wanted to lick it off, but as a woman of the world she knew how unseemly that would be. Instead, she wiped it clean in several passes with her ring finger and licked it from her fingertip until his upper lip was clean. Although Andrea had wanted to raise her glass in a toast with him ever since they had spotted the sausage stand, she refrained from doing so for now. She felt they were much further along in their relationship, and that to raise a toast to it now would be a step backwards (admittedly, it was the sort of thing she had often done in the past while feigning surprise at such proposals, even though she herself might have instigated them).

Atam made no move whatsoever to offer a toast. Satisfied, she sipped at her glass. She raised it higher than was absolutely necessary so she could swiftly fill her mouth. Glugging loudly, her eyes wide open, she swallowed noisily, the prominent whites of her eyes almost clown-like around her brown irises. She then lowered her glass, placed it loudly on the counter and, lady-like to a fault, refrained from wiping away the beer froth with the back of her hand. Instead, she gracefully angled her face towards him.

He understood instantly and, with his thumb, wiped the beer froth from her upper lip. She held her head between his hands and pushed against him, lifting her face towards his. But now her eyes grew even larger, even more clown-like, with tiny, delicate veins appearing in the whites. The alae of her nose quivered. Her upper lip trembled convulsively as she lustfully drew the corners of her mouth sideways and downwards, as if in agony.

Herr Kommerzialrat was the first to notice their intimacy. He clucked his tongue sharply and neatly, briefly raised his hat in salute and remarked, 'My compliments.' Andrea blushed to the roots of her hair and, giggling teasingly, buried her face in Atam's hands as the wind picked up, tousling her hair and bearing aloft a pile of litter and leaves.

Before the sausages and sauce cooled down completely, she turned from his embrace, graciously and apologetically. With the same familiar hand movement, she picked up a chunk of sausage from her plate and fed him. She then held up her fingers, sticky with sauce, for him to lick, which Atam did most obediently. In this way they finished off all the food, Andrea wiped both the plates clean with the leftover bread, which she fed alternately into his mouth and her own, giving a large portion of it to him. She herself ate only a little now and then, more to keep him company and chew along gracefully, thereby maintaining a certain commonality.

Andrea pushed the stacked plates around the corner towards the serving hatch. Sensing Atam's eyes on her back, she swivelled her hips more than was strictly necessary for the purpose of holding his attention. She angled her head towards her opposite shoulder as she did so. The sausage lady opened the hatch window to retrieve the plates, adding, 'That's very kind, thank you,' with the merest hint of a motherly smile.

Stepping back, Andrea propped up her hand by the tip of her middle finger, sliding it along the serving surface. Teasingly, she shortened her stride as she tiptoed away, peeling around the corner in a particularly showy manner, all of which Atam observed through the glass panels of the sausage stand. To please her, he feigned a startled surprise.

IV

Andrea suggested they take the No. 43 tram, alight two stops ahead and go to her apartment, but Atam objected that the police may already be watching their respective addresses. Fortunately, Andrea also had an uncle who lived in Vienna, out on Flötzersteig. He was a hut warden at the gamekeepers' college up on the pass near the footbridge. She was convinced there would almost certainly be a room for them and that no one would ever come looking for them way out there.

They tried and failed to hail a taxi. Either the taxi was already occupied or the driver was barrelling across the junction in the middle lane, trying to beat the flashing green of the traffic lights. Andrea thought about hitching up her skirt and showing her legs but decided against it as she couldn't be sure she hadn't laddered her tights leaping through the glass-tiled ceiling. And so, hand in hand, they continued walking south and crossed Rathauspark until they came up to a taxi rank on Stadiongasse in front of the parliament building. Atam opened the rear door for Andrea. She got in and slid over to make room for him who, in the meantime, had already walked around the back of the car to get in from the other side. Andrea then slid back over to the passenger side again just as Atam hurried back around the rear of the taxi to slip into the back seat. She thus slid back and forth on the seat trying to accommodate her companion on one side or the other.

They both burst out laughing at their antics. She rested her head on his shoulder and closed her eyes to narrow slits, sighing with pleasure as she noticed the driver scrutinising her legs in the rear-view mirror; indeed, they were now rather exposed from all the sliding back and forth across the back seat. She rubbed her knees together so her skirt, bunched up over her thighs, slid down sideways. She tugged at the hem of her skirt, pulling it upwards so the full length of her legs could be viewed unhindered in the rear-view mirror.

They drove out of town along Josefstädter Strasse, crossed the Gürtel orbital road in a succession of sharp bends and continued west along Ottakringer Strasse, past the eponymous brewery. Whenever the taxi braked, Andrea fell forward slightly, but Atam would tense his body and, with his arm on her waist, hold her back; her head would then fall forward, only to be tipped back again as the driver accelerated. She savoured these moments and allowed herself to sway back and forth even more. As they turned into Maroltingergasse, the taxi driver accelerated sharply to nip into a space in the cross traffic. Like a rag doll, Andrea was thrown against Atam, her knees flying up in the air and her skirt sliding right back as her mouth brushed against Atam's cheek. Atam held on to Andrea tightly, supporting her face with his, and tugged the hem of her skirt back down firmly, not without leaving his hand between her knees to make sure they remained covered. Andrea cooed.

She paid the fare but declined to tip the taxi driver as she felt he had been more than amply rewarded by the sight of her exposed legs. She led the way through the garden gate and exuberantly rang the bell three times as if it were a secret code, conveying a familiarity Atam was unsure whether or not to envy.

Once inside, Andrea introduced the two gentlemen and explained to Uncle László that they were on the run and needed a hideout as Atam was wanted by the police for murder. Atam nodded briefly as he introduced himself as 'Atam Prakash' and, to dispel any uncertainty (and clarify the situation, if only for Andrea's sake), added, 'It was an accident. A man was locked inside a room and somehow managed to kill himself in front of my eyes as he tried to shoot his way out of the door. All I wanted was to pick up these photos.' Atam extracted the photos from Andrea's bag as he spoke.

'Well, this certainly calls for a drink,' said the uncle, always on the lookout for a good excuse to break open a bottle of home-distilled schnapps. He shuffled off into the common room of the gamekeepers' college of Lower Austria and headed towards an old 1940s satin-wood sideboard. On display behind its yellowed crown-glass panes were all manner of fruit brandies; he reached for a hand-painted bottle of *Dirndlschnaps*, took out three pressed crystal goblets and proceeded to fill them to the rim.

'Oops!' the uncle remarked. He then raised his glass solemnly to eye level and, holding it out reverently towards Andrea and Atam, exclaimed, '*Egészségére*!' before tipping its contents down his throat, bending his knees slightly as he swallowed, bobbing up and down as he set the glass down, then groaning hoarsely as he did so. Andrea and Atam emptied their glasses in turn, Andrea emulating her uncle's movements albeit with less bobbing but a much higher and softer pitched groan. The uncle stretched his arm out towards Atam and said, 'We can now be on first name terms, Atam. Call me László.' He then proceeded to embrace Atam, kissing him on both cheeks.

So moved was Uncle László that he needed two more shots of schnapps to calm himself. His right leg kept twitching, which he sought to suppress by placing a hand on his knee. But as his leg was stronger than his hand, Uncle László as a whole now began to quiver. Andrea poured him two more glasses in quick succession; meanwhile, Atam tried to call Gretchen, but there was no answer. Presumably she would be sleeping right through the day as she recovered from the previous night. After messaging her to say he had the photographs, he began to look around the common room.

The tables and chairs were all made of beechwood, which made perfect sense given the location on the outskirts of the Vienna Woods. Hunting trophies hung on the walls. Arranged around the large stag antlers were roebuck horns and chamois sheaths; in between them, mouflon horns and heads of wild boar. Stuffed birds and martens were scattered into every available space. Just as Atam was turning his attention to the floor, Uncle László regained his composure and offered to show Andrea and Atam to their room.

Leading the way, he walked up a steep wooden staircase. Andrea followed, fleet of foot, continually catching up, then giggling as she paused, with Atam following at a more even pace keeping a short distance behind. László was now waiting up on the landing, grinning broadly and pointing down the narrow and short corridor at various chamber doors: 'The first room here is my room. Then there's the large guest room for the course instructors. And behind that is another small guest room.' With an amused look on his face he added, 'I'm not sure, shouldn't I give you separate rooms? After all, you're not married! Perhaps Atam should sleep in my room.' Andrea laughed girlishly and blushed. Atam was about to respond, but Uncle László beat him to it: 'Anyway, I need to go back downstairs now, there's a lecture by the Brigadier starting any moment now.'

Somewhat sheepishly yet expectantly, Andrea looked at Atam, allowing him to draw her close. She turned her head to the side shyly as he drew her in, her body language overly passive, and lowered her head, still flushed red from Uncle László's teasing. She allowed herself to fall against Atam slightly and remained there, leaning against him. As he held her by the waist and gently rested his chin on the crown of her head, she placed her arms around his hips, her heart pounding loudly. He could sense the odour of the dark plastic fibres of the fitted carpet, the flaking paint of the window frames, the cleaning agent that had dried on their cleaned panes, and the fragrance of Andrea's shampoo.

They heard the front door squeak open downstairs and the sounds of students chatting in the front garden drifted in. As the door closer slowly pulled it shut with a single metallic click, all was silent again. Cigarette smoke rose up the stairs, blending with the odour of window cleaner and carpet adhesive and the fragrance of washing detergent on Andrea's blouse.

Atam looked down into the front garden through the stained yet clean window pane and watched the students as they stood around waiting and smoking. Then a car pulled up, braking sharply at the garden gate, and an older-looking and rather stocky gentleman in a dark grey army uniform stepped out. He threw the car door shut and strode through the smokers, greeting them briefly as he did so, then opened the front door and disappeared inside. Atam heard the new arrival being greeted downstairs as Herr Brigadier. The Brigadier strode right through the vestibule, his boots creaking, drawing the smokers from the garden in his wake as they made their way towards the classroom. Up on the landing Atam again heard doors banging; then all was silent. As Andrea giggled softly, Atam became aware of her ever-widening eyes. The cigarette smoke had started to dispel, gradually ceding sovereignty once again to the window cleaner, carpet adhesive and Andrea's deodorant.

Andrea felt behind her for the door handle and opened it. Swaying her hips, she pulled Atam into the room with her, their faces still pressed together; eventually, they reached the bedside. Leaning over gently, they allowed themselves to fall onto the soft and receptive surface, their lips briefly losing contact as they fell sideways onto the bed, only to let their mouths seek each other again after the bounce. Half buried under Atam, Andrea wiggled her lower legs to shake off her shoes. Her eyes grew large as she did so, deep furrows appearing on her brow. As her calves rhythmically struck the edge of the bed, Andrea involuntarily withdrew her lips from

Atam's, who eagerly sought them again, the ensuing interplay giving Andrea great pleasure, so much so that even after her feet were bare, she continued her kicking motion until Atam turned over in a flash and picked her up; she surrendered and came to lie sprawled over him.

At that moment they heard loud applause coming up from the classroom on the ground floor. They paused briefly, staring at each other, barely able to stifle their giggles. He carefully brushed the hair out of her face, tucking it behind her coquettishly protruding ears, then ran his finger down along her neck in a single continuous movement, casually undoing the top buttons of her blouse. Andrea's eyes widened even further as she felt her breath taken away. She gulped and silently moved her lips as if trying to utter something, then swallowed hard once again. Atam swallowed too as Andrea now ran her fingers through his hair, supporting herself on the bed with only one hand, causing her body to arch and her breasts, now barely covered by the half-open blouse, to hover over his face. Andrea reached up and slipped off her suit jacket. Atam, ever the gentleman, helped her out of it and laid the jacket out neatly beside him on the bed.

She closed her eyes, now so big, and this time arched only her neck upwards, as if inviting Atam to bite deep into her throat and drink the blood from her throbbing artery. He ran his hand under the open blouse and unfastened the clasp of her bra. Then he took a deep breath and declared his feelings for her, whispering breathlessly into her ear, whereupon she broke down with a scream and began to wail terribly. As she shook convulsively, her nose began to run and she shyly yet nimbly wiped it with the back of her hand, momentarily halting her sobbing. She stared at Atam wide-eyed and overjoyed and then began to mewl with embarrassment. Stopping suddenly and puffing with quivering lips, she then resumed her howling bitterly and most miserably.

Atam was initially startled and taken aback by this reaction, and it was only when she again smiled at him with tears in her eyes that he understood that Andrea was desperately eager to share her shock and emotion with him. Atam began dabbing at Andrea's tears as they ran down her cheeks and collected on her chin. By then, her eyelids were smudged dark with the mascara dissolved by her tears, yet never had she looked more adorable and vulnerable. As he hugged her, she regained her composure and once again began to breathe calmly and evenly.

V

The next day, the ceiling light was still on when the Brigadier knocked softly at the bedroom door, opening it just a crack to peer inside and see if anyone was awake. After discussing the matter with the caretaker, the previous day, he had agreed with Uncle László that he would take the couple to the Allentsteig military training unit in his comfortable company car – a Mercedes no less. Uncle László, no doubt still under the influence of residual alcohol, had hugged the Brigadier, something the latter had gruffly rebuffed, saying the only kisses he might accept were László's niece's. Uncle László had staggered backwards, laughed out loud – embarrassed and honoured at the same time! And added that that could certainly be arranged, given all the women in Andrea's family were keen on men in uniforms.

And so, the Brigadier pushed the bedroom door open and, as was bound to happen, Andrea woke up that very instant. One would wonder whether she had heard the door creak as it was being opened or simply felt instinctively that someone was staring at her. In any case, she looked through her huge eyes and, rather girlishly, whispered a barely audible

'Good morning,' involuntarily sitting up in such a way that her breasts softly touched Atam's face as he slept. She smiled at the Brigadier, her overly long eyelashes still blinking sleepily.

The Brigadier quietly stepped into the room, his index finger up at his lips, causing Andrea to chuckle softly and conspiratorially. He whispered that he was offering to take her with him as far as Allentsteig, in keeping with her uncle's request. Andrea blushed and nodded complicitly. The Brigadier remained very still as if hoping to halt time itself. She inhaled so deeply that her breasts were presented fully; then, just as slowly, she exhaled again, allowing her breasts to sink back down against Atam's face. She held the Brigadier's gaze as she did so, blushing even more.

The Brigadier knelt quietly before her, again holding his finger up to his lips; with a whisper, he asked whether she would definitely be coming along too. Andrea offered up an even wider smile than before and nodded vigorously, her hair falling like shadows across Atam's face. She raised her lower right leg in emphasis and it rose upwards from the bed like a soft and slender flagstaff. The Brigadier reached out his hand towards her. 'Promise?' he enquired softly. She nodded again, replying, 'Promise,' and placed her hand on his. The Brigadier mimed a kiss on the back of her hand before letting it go. With both holding their index fingers up to their lips, he slowly stepped backwards out of the room.

Andrea let her lower leg drop back down onto the bed and, with excited anticipation at the day ahead, drummed her shins on the bed, immediately rousing Atam from his slumber. Wide-eyed with excitement, she told him that the Brigadier would be taking them to Allentsteig in his limousine, that Uncle László had arranged it all and that they needed to hurry.

She sat herself down at the little bureau by the window and meticulously brushed her hair, alternately gazing pensively out of the window through the yellowed macramé curtains and staring just as pensively at a corner of the room. Atam asked her what was on her mind. She replied that she was still sleepy but coffee would definitely wake her up. She gave him a rather forced smile, or so it seemed to him. While he tied his shoelaces, she applied fresh mascara over the one stained by yesterday's tears of joy. She felt it would be appropriate for her appearance today to wear a somewhat tragic look. The whole time she glanced repeatedly at a small compact mirror she had folded out from an old-fashioned gilded box.

The table had been set for three, but the Brigadier had already finished his breakfast. 'He's upstairs in his room packing his things,' said Uncle László. 'What do you think? Wasn't it rather clever of me to set things up for you? Nowhere is the rabbit safer than in the lion's den,' he added as he cleared away the dirty porcelain plate with traces of strawberry jam and an apple core. Andrea stared at the breakfast leftovers that Uncle László was removing from the plate in front of her, as if seeking tangible evidence that Herr Brigadier had indeed already finished his breakfast, that he really did exist and that he really would be chauffeuring Andrea.

She was smiling as she watched the plate with the leftovers of the Brigadier's breakfast being taken away. Still smiling, she raised her eyebrows self-assuredly, giving herself a rather arrogant yet delightfully confident look, and then took a deep breath before uttering a loud sigh. She let Atam pour her some coffee and crossed her legs as she waited for him to add milk and sugar before stirring the beverage. Her little grey skirt had slipped back up again and so, with an ostensible display of bashfulness, she tugged at the hem of her skirt to pull it down an immeasurably short distance. She then stretched out her right leg for an instant, displaying her little silver ankle chain and admiring it complacently.

She drank her coffee, in many small sips interspersed with deliberately long and meaningful pauses, all the while letting her gaze wander restlessly around the room without alighting anywhere in particular. Her wide eyes seemed introspective. Atam prepared two slices of bread and butter and added slices of sausage and cheese. He placed one on Andrea's plate in front of her. She thanked him but explained that she did not wish to eat anything as she was keen to stay slim.

VI

Atam prepared two more sandwiches and wrapped them in serviettes as snacks for the journey. Andrea, reluctant to put them inside her little bag, waved them away with a dismissive gesture, frowning disapprovingly, and so, Atam proceeded to eat both sandwiches. He was keen to avoid drawing attention to himself again with his rumbling stomach. Andrea was inspecting her fingernails while sipping her second cup of coffee when heavily booted footsteps were heard coming down the stairs. As if waiting for his cue, Uncle László hurried into the room just ahead of the Brigadier to hold the door open for him. 'I believe you've already become acquainted,' said Uncle László by way of introductions; Andrea chuckled, looking sheepishly at the Brigadier and blushing to the roots of her hair.

Outside, a car could be heard pulling up at the garden gate. There was a knock at the door of the common room and a driver in uniform entered and nodded politely, his cursory surveying glance ultimately lingering on Andrea's knees. They all went out to the car, and the Brigadier relieved Andrea of her small bag from her willingly extended hand and placed it alongside his suitcase on the passenger seat. He then opened the rear door for her, allowing her to get in and move over to the middle seat while Atam walked around the car, opened his own rear door behind the driver and got in. Meanwhile, the Brigadier had taken his seat next to Andrea.

The chauffeur drove off at an ostentatiously slow pace, but in order to filter his way into the sheer endless column of early morning traffic on Flötzersteig, he was forced to accelerate harder. So even before the travelling party had managed to settle comfortably in the back of the limousine and fasten their seatbelts, they were all thrown to one side, Andrea squealing with surprise as she landed with her head on the Brigadier's shoulder, both her breasts bumping against his chest. The Brigadier gulped loudly enough for Andrea to hear despite the roar of the engine. She manoeuvred her feet over the transmission hump and into the Brigadier's footwell, as if bracing herself for further vehicular lurching. She placed her foot with the ankle chain so close to the Brigadier's foot that both feet were now touching. She cast a furtive glance at him, flashing him a smile that pierced him to the core. Atam reached for Andrea's hand so he could steady her as he had done already the previous day, but today Andrea did not let him hold her hand; instead, she placed both hands on her lap and held herself securely.

Again, Andrea found herself in the line of sight of a driver's rear-view mirror and, the driver adjusted the mirror again, ostensibly to avoid her gaze but in reality, to see more of her legs. She in turn glanced in the rear-view mirror, confirming her feeling of being eyed. The Brigadier started a conversation with Andrea by asking her about their journey's destination.

She informed him that they were eager to get out of Vienna temporarily as Atam had incidentally witnessed an accident and that they were eager to drop below the radar in order to avoid being implicated. As she spoke, the Brigadier tentatively ran the tip of his foot across her instep, as if by accident. She did not flinch; rather, she returned the favour, likewise stroking the back of his foot with her toe. As she did so, she opened her knees slightly, a move she noticed the driver had also spotted. Andrea smiled at him in the rear-view mirror and pulled down the corners of her mouth, as if in pain.

And they drove west down Flötzersteig, making slow progress down a traffic lane constricted by cycle routes, past the cemetery, and were continually held up by the raised zebra crossings. At the first such crossing, the driver had been distracted looking at Andrea's legs in the rear-view mirror and was forced to brake far too late and abruptly, propelling all the passengers' forwards against their seatbelts. Andrea grasped the seatbelt stretched tightly across her breasts and loosened its grip by throwing herself against the backrest. She puffed and blew heavily as she did so, pulling down the corners of her mouth once again, as if in agony, and nodded knowingly and eagerly at the Brigadier, drawing his attention towards her breasts, a vulnerably delicate and feminine yearning for his protection.

The Brigadier admonished the driver harshly to pay more attention and, to fill the ensuing silence, began to talk about how he had often driven from the military training area to the Czech Republic, even back in the days of the Iron Curtain. On his first time ever, he had taken a coach from Vienna to Telč and then a guided tour through the old town. They had dined at the inn on the market square and a waitress had made eyes at him. He had been convinced ever since that he would one day marry a foreigner. In the short pause that the Brigadier took as if to catch his breath, Andrea enquired whether he was indeed married. He shook his head vigorously, uttering aloud, 'Oh, my goodness, no!' As an aside, he added that the waitress had not been in Andrea's league by any stretch of imagination and that, much later on, when he had been in command of the unit at Kaisersteinbruch and had often shopped in Sopron, he had resolved that if he were ever to marry at all, it would be to a Hungarian woman. At this point, Andrea enquired whether the Brigadier was so fickle a man that he kept falling in love with all manner of foreign women. The Brigadier sighed and stated that he was a one-woman man and that if and when he fell in love, it would be forever.

Andrea blushed to the roots of her hair, exhaled deeply and furrowed her brow most dramatically. The Brigadier went on to say that he had had a Hungarian dictionary ever since and had always intended to learn the language but had never taken the time to do so until now. Andrea replied that his pronunciation of *Sopron* had been flawless, like a true Hungarian; she even enquired whether he had Hungarian ancestors. The Brigadier shook his head, saying that he didn't know but that he had always been attracted to the *puszta*, not just because of the military training area near the border but also because of its desolate landscape and the impenetrable border behind which Hungary lay like a land beyond—unknown and foreign, yet so close and familiar, as if viewed through a veil.

As the limousine accelerated up the motorway slip road near Auhof and the engine howled, everyone fell silent, and it was only at the top, beyond the sharp right-hand bend on the crest of the carriageway, that the automatic transmission shifted into a higher gear and the engine calmed the momentum of the higher revs into a smooth yet perceptible acceleration. The Brigadier then asked Andrea where she had been born and how was it that she came to live in Vienna. Before answering, she gave a slight pout, a look which, combined with her big round eyes, was most harmonious, and then swallowed hard. In a clear and rather melodic voice, she explained that she had grown up in Valkó, a village right next to Gödöllö, and that after graduating school the same year the Iron Curtain fell, she had been referred by her sports teacher to the Bohemian Prater amusement park in Vienna to work as an assistant in a shooting gallery at a time when she did not speak a word of German. 'So, you see, Brigadier, I know my way around guns. And just so you know: I shoot like a sniper, too.'

Andrea pursed her lips, furrowed her brow and then tugged her skirt towards her knees once again. She then leaned back and asked, 'What kind of Brigadier are you anyway, Herr Brigadier?' The Brigadier replied that he was a Brigadier general, in other words, a mere one-star general from the Third Brigade of Hunters and that he, personally, was not a good shot. At this, he reached up and loosened his tie and undid his top shirt button. 'You don't mind, do you?' he asked Andrea as he did so. She nodded eagerly, adding, 'You might as well undo the next button, too,' all the while stroking the Brigadier's foot with the tips of her shoes.

Atam had fallen asleep as early on as Hadikgasse, his head leaning against the padded C-pillar. He now woke up, beset with nausea, observing Andrea as she cosied up to the Brigadier. He coughed rather hysterically and, after a pause for dramatic effect, opened his eyes and slowly turned his head towards Andrea. And sure enough, she halted the play she was making with the Brigadier and looked at him innocently. 'My apologies,' said Atam. 'I always tend to feel rather sick when I'm sitting in the back of large limousines. Would you mind if we stopped for a moment so I can stretch my legs in the fresh air and then I'll go and sit in the front?'

As he paced up and down the hard shoulder, he phoned Gretchen. She answered immediately, saying, 'At last! Thank goodness you've called! I've been on tenterhooks here. I need to know how it all went. Have you got the photos?' 'Well, I did call right afterwards, but you didn't answer,' Atam replied apologetically. 'I didn't sleep a wink all night,' Gretchen replied angrily. 'I only fell asleep after you'd left and then I slept through. I've been on pins and needles ever since. Thank goodness you texted me at least.' 'Yes, I've got the photos, but that's not all. I couldn't text you the most important thing or the police would have had it in writing if our phones are being tapped. Harmstedter's dead.' 'But you've got the photos, right? All of them?' 'I don't know which ones you wanted. I've got all the photos he had on him. But there's nothing on them that could bother you. Just trees.' 'Well, that's a typical comment only a man would make. Of course, there are trees on it. But you need to realise the sensuality with which I photographed those trees. Anyone with eyes in their head would realise I was totally in love when I took them.' 'With me, right?' 'Of course, my love. That's why it had to be you who got those photos for me. After all, it's all your fault.' 'Harmstedter shot himself trying to shoot open the glass doors to let me in.' 'That sounds like something he would do. I'm so glad I divorced him. Listen, I need to get something to eat, I'm all in shock. Call me later, or better still, bring the pictures round right away and come and comfort your new widow.' 'It's not a good idea for us to see each other right now; the police could be looking for me.' 'What's more important is that you come and comfort me. It's what I need right now. You know, honey, matters of the heart – it's what counts.' And with that, she hung up.

Atam went and sat in the front with the driver so they could continue the journey and passed the Brigadier's briefcase and Andrea's handbag towards the back of the car. He left his window open a crack, the rush of the incoming wind helping him to distract himself from the conversation in the back seat.

As they drove past Pressbaum in the Vienna Woods, Andrea resumed the conversation. Leaning in towards the Brigadier and speaking in a quiet voice, she said she would be interested to know whether the driver was also the Brigadier's private secretary, readily conceding that the question was actually none of her business. The Brigadier replied that he didn't even have a secretary; all he had to do was request transport and his office booked a car complete with driver, male or female. Andrea briefly interjected that, if she had any say in the matter, the Brigadier would be assigned male drivers exclusively as she would not want him to be seduced by the legs of a female chauffeur; after all, a woman's legs behind the wheel were particularly seductive, as long as they were reasonably shapely, of course.

It was now the Brigadier's turn to blush and, once again, he stressed the fact that he was absolutely a one-woman man and quietly made the solemn promise never to let himself be driven by a female chauffeur. He underscored his sincerity by running his foot upwards along Andrea's calf while she glanced at him sideways, casting a delphine look. She believed him.

Andrea, feeling she could always believe every word the Brigadier said, gave a resigned sigh and shook her head as if to negate some thought or other, and her eyes widened. 'Wonderful,' Andrea said to the Brigadier. 'Your wife, your future wife, will appreciate that very much, and I'm absolutely certain she will repay you with the same attention.' The Brigadier was about to say something in reply, but Andrea mischievously placed her index finger to her lips just as the two of them had done earlier in the guest bedroom.

'What else are you planning to do today once we reach Allentsteig?' Andrea asked in the pause that ensued. 'Brigadier?' 'Peter,' the Brigadier replied. 'Please call me Peter.' Andrea responded that it was not her place to do so, but if it made the Brigadier happy, she would address him as Peter. 'And how may I address you?' the Brigadier asked in return. 'My name's Andrea, but you already know that, don't you, Peter?' she replied with a teasingly malicious smile.

'Would you like me to answer your question now, Andrea?' the Brigadier enquired. Andrea replied that she would always want Peter to answer all her questions. He gulped, nodding emphatically, and obediently proceeded to describe what he had in mind: on arrival, he was going to dine at an old inn in the neighbouring village after walking through the forest to get there, at which point Andrea sighed and added that a hike would be wonderful. He went on to explain that they had the best potato dumplings there, made from raw and cooked potatoes, and again Andrea protested that she was perfectly familiar with the recipe and that she could make it herself since, originally, it was after all a Hungarian recipe. The Brigadier went on to say that he never drank alcohol but that with this dish of Hungarian dumplings – '*Gombóc,*' Andrea interjected, blinking complicitly with both eyes, which were always so expressive on account of her long eyelashes. '*Gombóc,*' she repeated, pulling her short skirt forward again, 'is the Hungarian word.' '*Gombóc,*' repeated the Brigadier, adding 'With these *gombóc,*' – 'Beautifully pronounced, Peter, like a true hussar,' interrupted Andrea once again – 'With these *gombóc* and roast pork,' the Brigadier continued, 'Nothing beats a good Czech beer.'

'And after the *gombóc* with roast pork? What will you do then, Peter?' asked Andrea mercilessly. 'Then,' replied the Brigadier, 'I'll get lost on the way back to the barracks because my thoughts will be entirely elsewhere.' Andrea asked where the Brigadier might be at that point in his thoughts. She pretended to believe he might be thinking about the briefing or the innkeeper's granddaughter. The Brigadier sighed heavily but did not respond.

Andrea instantly pulled her foot away from him, shaking her head disapprovingly and pursing her lips. Her raised eyebrows wrinkled her rather clammy forehead, but in the most delightful way, as she stared fixedly out of the car window on her side. The Brigadier soon relented and, between his teeth, whispered that Andrea knew fully well that he would be thinking of her and that, in fact, he had not been able to think of anything else since that morning.

Andrea rewarded the Brigadier by immediately placing her hand on his arm and turning to face him again. But then she quickly withdrew her hand, putting her index finger up to her lips and whispering that such gestures were forbidden, absolutely forbidden: she was, after all, already taken.

The Brigadier began to sob quietly, shaking as he did so, but did not contradict her, something that displeased Andrea, who was now staring straight ahead through the windscreen. She held her raised eyebrows remarkably high, giving her a rather haughty look and creasing her brow yet again, her lips pursed as if she were about to spit out cherry stones.

This state of affairs prevailed from Langenrohr beyond the Tulln bypass and across the new bridge over the Danube all the way to the slip road onto the new motorway that ran alongside the Danube. It was at this point that the chauffeur rather misjudged the lateral centrifugal forces at work in the spiralling curve and Andrea's foot struck the Brigadier's shin sharply. 'I'm so sorry,' whispered Andrea. The Brigadier quickly grabbed her knee and held it firmly. She gave the Brigadier a conspiratorial look and allowed his hand to rest on her knee all the way from Utzenlaa to Frauendorf. Then, with a graceful but deliberate movement, she brushed his massaging hand off her knee, ran the back of her hand fleetingly along his wrist and, negatively shaking her head, she looked him straight in the face. She whispered that, while his chauffeurs had in the past no doubt witnessed a great deal, it would undoubtedly be better if the two of them waited until they were undisturbed – unless of course he would prefer it if someone were watching.

'Andrea, really!' the Brigadier pleaded. She briefly shrugged her shoulders, rolled her eyes and with the voice of innocence asked what the big deal was. The Brigadier was at a loss for words and looked around uneasily, wanting to say something. Andrea put her finger to her lips yet again and smiled until the Brigadier acquiesced and fell silent.

At Fels am Wagram, the chauffeur left the Danube motorway and took the B34 to Horn. In Hadersdorf am Kamp, the Brigadier asked in a whisper what they should do. Andrea whispered back innocently, 'What do you mean, "do"?' The Brigadier replied that they could not carry on like this and that the journey would be over in three quarters of an hour if they did not go and eat something on the way. Andrea replied that the Brigadier was a man and ought to know what needs to be done; he was after all a Brigadier. He replied that he knew very well what needed to be done and what he wanted; what he didn't know was what Andrea really wanted. She replied that he must surely be capable of seeing what she wanted and anyway ought to feel it deep within his heart – that 'nothing ventured nothing gained'. And that, if it wasn't too much to ask, it was up to him to do the right thing; after all, she herself was merely a weak and helpless woman caught up in a man's world.

In Langenlois, the Brigadier asked Andrea if she would consider becoming his personal assistant and offered to hire her on the spot so she could decide in peace and quiet by his side how best to proceed, adding she would have to accept immediately; otherwise, he would simply have to kidnap her. Andrea's face had clouded over at the mention of the job offer, but the promise of a potential abduction was sufficiently flattering for her to accept for the time being. And so, she briefly took the Brigadier's hand, squeezed it tightly, dug her fingernails so deep into his skin that the nail marks turned dark purple, and answered frivolously, 'Yes, I do!' before withdrawing her hand again.

Just before Gars am Kamp, the Brigadier asked Andrea whether she would now like to eat something. She replied that a short break in the journey would certainly be nice and a bite to eat would be wonderful, so the Brigadier ordered the driver to stop at the Goldener Hirsch on the main square. Gazelle-like, Andrea leapt out of the car along with the Brigadier and, twirling her hips girlishly with every step, walked beside him towards the tavern entrance, giving way to the Brigadier as they reached the door and then waited for Atam. The chauffeur remained in the car.

Thanks to the Brigadier's uniform, they instantly caught the landlord's attention. He ushered them over to the regulars' table, immediately removing the ornate metal sign with the inscription *Stammtisch* from its centre. Andrea took her seat, now in her capacity as Frau Brigadier. A waiter quickly brought over two large beers and one small one, and Andrea proceeded to raise a toast to her new position. Atam, of course, had not been privy to these developments while seated in the front passenger seat; all he knew was that this time, he would have to wipe the beer foam from his lips himself with the back of his own hand.

'So, what do you think of that, Atam?' asked Andrea. 'Isn't it great I've found a new job so quickly? I'm starting right away!' Andrea, her eyes wide open, explained that she would now need to send Atam back to Vienna so he could pack some things for her from her apartment and then forward them to her as she would now be staying in Allentsteig for a while, taking dictations for the Brigadier's new book. What a stroke of luck that the Brigadier had been planning to commit to paper the wealth of experience he had acquired on his many manoeuvres.

While they read the menus, the Brigadier and Andrea exchanged telephone numbers and sent each other their first text messages, laughing somewhat coyly and pointing out how easy and complicated at the same time it had become now to communicate. Andrea managed to send the Brigadier a kiss icon without Atam noticing. She then made her choice of food known to the Brigadier, excused herself, stood up and disappeared to the Ladies'.

Not long after, the Brigadier's phone signalled an incoming message, so he briefly put down his menu to check it. Instantly, the blood rushed to his face as the screen showed Andrea in front of the mirror in the ladies', blowing a kiss to the camera. He quickly slid his phone under the menu as Andrea strode back to the table, her lips pursed, her clothes neat and tidy, and her hair combed, everyone reverently stepping aside for her, not wanting to risk any contretemps with the army.

The meal passed off in silence, except that Andrea kept nudging the Brigadier to talk about his book project. Even before the Brigadier had used up all his best anecdotes, he waved to the landlord to bring the bill. The Brigadier, fully in command of the whole situation, gave a breezy gesture of his hand and walked out in silence, heading towards the chauffeur, who immediately started the engine.

Between Gars and Rosenburg, Andrea arranged herself so she could sit with her legs crossed, tugging her skirt down as far as it would go. From Rosenburg to Horn, she propped herself up with both hands on the seat, fatigued and sleepy from the meal. In Horn, it occurred to her that she should write down some instructions for Atam.

With the notepad bearing the *Bundesheer* army letterhead already on her lap, Andrea took the ballpoint pen and clicked it. She scrutinised the beautiful silver Parker Sonnet and, after examining the fine engraving, read it aloud. She hesitated for a moment when she got to '60th birthday', a wicked smile appearing fleetingly on her beautiful face, then read the rank of Brigadier General and his surname Nemecek out loud, a very Slovakian name, all the while playing footsie with him.

She first wrote down her address, then sketched out the layout of her apartment. She giggled inwardly when she realised the outline of her flat would not fit on one page, so she tore off the top sheet of paper and continued drawing on the next page. Then she began to compile a to-do list, numbering each item. She tilted her head erratically towards one shoulder and then forwards so her loose hair hung like a curtain in front of her face, concealing the play of her lips as she silently mumbled the individual items to herself. Occasionally, she would push her hair back behind her ear using the pushbutton of the ballpoint pen, then carry on writing, holding the pen between her index and middle fingers, pointing the tip towards herself and writing along her thigh. Whenever she paused, she would bring the pen up to her lips and put its pushbutton into her mouth as she pulled the corners of her mouth downwards, again as if in some sort of pain.

In Göpfritz an der Wild, the Brigadier asked the chauffeur whether he would be prepared, for a fee, to drive Atam back to Vienna that same day after his shift was over and then drive the lady's luggage back up to the military training area? 'Yes, sir,' said the chauffeur, nodding. Andrea suppressed a huge sigh of relief and grasped the Brigadier's arm in exuberant gratitude as she casually, almost unintentionally, slipped the ballerina shoe off her right foot and stroked his shin with the ball of her foot, which was covered only by a thin stocking, wiggling her toes enticingly as she did so.

They turned onto a gravel road that was unrutted even though, evidently, it was frequently used; in a strange way it seemed rather forlorn here in the forest. Once again, the chauffeur's braggadocio came to the fore in his unbearably slow driving pace, so much so that Atam was wondering whether he would soon be pulling a lever inside the glove compartment and two small pennants would rise up from the wings of the limousine, bearing the regimental standard and the Austrian flag fluttering in the wind. But at that moment, they halted in front of a barrier and the driver switched off the engine.

A guard stepped up to the car, saluted the Brigadier, checked his ID and then raised the barrier. The driver drove on and let the limousine glide across the compound at walking pace before stopping in front of the officers' wing. The Brigadier took his leave of Atam, stepped out of the car and walked slowly towards the entrance, where he then waited with his suitcase and Andrea's bag in his hand.

VII

They had not yet had the opportunity to talk things over and, as he grabbed Andrea by the waist, she defensively placed her hands on his forearms pushing him back softly. She sought to assume an air of desperation that she felt would seem appropriate for the situation. And indeed, she succeeded in letting a few tears trickle down over the grey traces of dried mascara from yesterday's outburst of happiness. She then twirled around coyly before walking up to the Brigadier so Atam could just about spot the tears she had managed to conjure up. She felt a great deal of joy and satisfaction at this achievement. Through the rear window of the departing vehicle, Atam watched Andrea make her entrance into the building, and he breathed a sigh of relief that he had been released from this bizarre affair so briefly and painlessly – or so he thought at the time.

The early evening traffic had clogged up the Nordbrücke bridge and the Gürtelbrücke was closed due to road works, contributing in part to the traffic jam on the Nordbrücke. And so, they crossed at the Reichsbrücke instead and, coming down Lassallestrasse, drove three quarters of a full circle around Admiral Tegetthoff's Bronze Monument, the driver saluting him and grinning as he did so. They continued along the quayside boulevard, then on across Schottenring, past the former Creditanstalt bank building, across Universitätsstrasse into Alserstrasse to the Winter coffeehouse. Andrea's apartment was located there, in the same Gründerzeit building.

The chauffeur was eager to get a table at the coffeehouse and have some dinner while Atam went upstairs to collect some of Andrea's things from her apartment. Indeed, Atam scampered up the staircase several steps at a time and, barely out of breath, exited the stairwell on the second floor and walked down the corridor, past the windows looking out into the courtyard he had just crossed. The window niches opposite the apartment doors had small DIY shelving units and discarded sideboards filled with pots growing chives, ferns and geraniums.

He stopped in front of door No. 13 and put the key to the lock, but it would not go in. He used his other hand as a support under the key, but even with both hands the result was still the same. Next, he tried to insert the main entrance door key – after all, perhaps he had got the keys mixed up? But the entrance door key did not fit either. He became nervous and began to feel guilty towards the driver, whose spare time he was now pointlessly wasting by keeping him downstairs in the coffeehouse instead of allowing him to go home.

Atam tried to phone the driver, but there was no answer. Perhaps he had just nipped to the Gents, thought Atam. So, he turned around and walked back out to the street and entered Kaffee Winter to look for the driver. He checked all the tables, but the driver was nowhere to be seen. He asked the waitress for directions to the Gents. He followed her past the serving counter towards the kitchen entrance and, as instructed by her, turned into a corridor that had many doors leading off it. The first one was marked 'PRIVATE' in black letters; the second, 'EMERGENCY EXIT'; the last one, finally, was the Gents.

There was no one at the urinals, and even though the lingering odour might have indicated otherwise, he could tell from the open cubicle doors that none was occupied. So, there was no need to call out the driver's name. Atam left the Gents and, after a moment's hesitation, turned towards the Ladies. Perhaps the driver had made a mistake or been caught rather short and had decided to relieve himself in the ladies' toilets? Anything was possible, Atam told himself, as he pushed open the door to the Ladies. A woman was standing at a wash basin, rinsing her hands. Filling the room was a fug of faecal odours blending with the fragrance of perfume and soap.

Atam said hello and excused himself by saying he was looking for someone. He then asked the woman whether a gentleman had perhaps suddenly appeared in the Ladies, but she did not answer. Atam stepped up to the first cubicle and pushed open the door. It was warm but empty, and the cistern was refilling. He stepped over to the second cubicle, but it was locked. Atam knocked and asked whether the driver was in there but received no answer. Instead, the woman who had been washing her hands pointed out as she was leaving that there was a sign on the cubicle door that said 'Out of order'. Atam left the toilets and walked out through the emergency exit, finding himself in the hallway of the street-side wing of Andrea's apartment building. He went back up to her apartment and tried both the keys again and, rather pointlessly, his own keys, which he had found in his trouser pocket. None of the keys would fit.

Andrea answered her phone right away as if she had been waiting for his call. He wasn't sure, after all, how to address her on the phone, so he simply said that the keys didn't fit the lock and that the driver had disappeared. Then, after a short pause, he asked how she was and whether she was safe.

Andrea was very surprised by it all. Especially by his question; after all, she now belonged to the army too and was protected and guarded by several regiments at her current location. She then asked him whether he had tried both the keys and had pulled the door firmly towards himself into its frame before unlocking it just as she had described in her instructions. Atam explained that he hadn't even got that far since the keys didn't fit. She suppressed a loud and rather vulgar chuckle, then substituted it for something more ladylike as she asked Atam to hang on while she searched her handbag.

Andrea blew her nose. Then he heard an unintelligible male voice, probably the Brigadier's, ask her something, and she replied, purringly, that she would be right there and was just looking quickly for something in her handbag. He heard a giggle. Then all was quiet except for the metallic sounds emanating from her handbag as she rummaged around. Andrea found her keys and confirmed to Atam that the keys he had could not possibly fit. In her understandable excitement, she had accidentally given him the office keys. But they couldn't talk on the phone right now as the Brigadier needed her. She asked him what she should do now that she didn't have her things but ended up answering her own question. 'I'll see what I can do, but I have to go now.' She cautiously blew him a kiss over the phone and hung up without waiting for Atam's response.

As he made his way back down to the coffeehouse on the ground floor of the building, he wondered where he was going to lay low for the night if he couldn't get into Andrea's apartment. Before he settled at a table, he walked through the entire premises once again; perhaps the driver had re-emerged in the meantime? There were plenty of reasons why he might have been delayed. Perhaps he had forgotten something in the car that he would need over dinner: some medicine or his phone; perhaps he had just popped out to buy some cigarettes or a magazine to pass the time.

But once again the driver was nowhere to be seen. And this time the waitress barred his way, telling him he couldn't just keep coming in and out and going to the toilet but had to consume something beforehand if he wanted to use the Gents; after all, the toilets were there for the restaurant's patrons and this was not a public convenience. Again, Atam explained that he was genuinely looking for his driver, just as he had done earlier, and that he really did want to eat something. He added that he had not used the toilets earlier on: all he had done was go and look to see if his driver was there as he had not seen him sitting anywhere in the restaurant, which was where they had agreed to meet.

But Atam's honest and genuine answer fell on deaf ears as the waitress angrily retorted that he should perish the thought that he could pull the wool over her eyes just because she was a woman and that she would immediately call her boss if he did not scarper instantly. Just as Atam was searching for a solid rejoinder to try and appease the waitress, the driver entered the coffeehouse from Alserstrasse. As he caught sight of Atam, he waved excitedly across the restaurant towards the bar counter at the back where the stand-off between Atam and the waitress was taking place and hurried towards them. 'Look,' Atam said to the waitress triumphantly. 'Here comes my chauffeur.' By then the driver had reached Atam and was apologising casually and somewhat complicitly, explaining with a nod and a wink that, instead of dining at the restaurant, he had preferred to call in on a female acquaintance; at this, he gave him a vulgar grin. Atam looked bemused, so the driver gave his shoulder a slight shove, adding, 'You get my drift, don't you? I mean, that was a bit of a babe you had with you earlier on yourself.'

By now the waitress had had enough of it all and yelled at both the driver and Atam to take their amorous affairs elsewhere and extract themselves from the premises that instant or she would call her boss and he would know how to deal with the likes of them. Atam, however, pushed the waitress aside and rushed ahead of the driver into the WC corridor and out through the emergency exit into the vestibule of Andrea's building.

In the courtyard, Atam waited for the driver, who arrived clapping his hands and shouting 'Respect!' Once he had caught up with Atam in the courtyard, he patted him on the shoulder in a friendly way, still full of praise, saying, 'Not bad, man, not bad.' Atam burst through the entrance doorway and told the driver that he had been handed the office keys instead of the apartment keys by mistake. The driver then asked Atam whether he had somewhere to stay the night. If not, he could come back to his girlfriend's place and spend the night on the sofa in the living room.

Atam thanked the driver but said that he preferred not to stray too far from the apartment as he expected a spare key to be delivered at some point. The driver shook his head and explained that his acquaintance lived just around the corner and that, in fact, her windows might even give onto the same courtyard. Atam relented and gratefully accepted the offer, provided it was no trouble and that his acquaintance agreed. 'Oh absolutely,' said the driver. 'She loves meeting new men. I'm Fritz, by the way,' he added, holding out his hand to Atam.

The driver led the way, half-a-step ahead of Atam, but obligingly half-turned towards him as he walked. They turned into Brünnlbadgasse, crossed Mariannengasse and turned east into Gilgegasse. After just a few steps, they stopped in front of a forged iron gate with glass panels behind floral embellishments that offered a view into the marble-clad entrance hall. Atam wondered how one could possibly look out from a building on Gilgegasse across a courtyard to a building on Alserstrasse and resolved to take the driver's descriptions of locations less literally in future.

VIII

They went up the stairs to the second floor, its corridor offering a view of a large ash tree in the rear courtyard, and stopped in front of door No. 13. The driver opined with a smile that thirteen had actually been a lucky number but that it had been discredited by the envious out of sheer jealousy. Atam politely agreed and said that while the number of Andrea's apartment was also thirteen, it had not brought him much luck when he was standing in front of its door without a key. 'Who can say?' responded Fritz, adding that Atam might perhaps even take a shine to his acquaintance and that they could do a swap.

Before Atam could object, the door was opened and a petite woman with blond hair that was in fact light brown at the roots stood there in front of them in a bathrobe. She appeared surprised and pulled the bathrobe tighter across her cleavage as she caught sight of Atam while smiling at him in obvious amusement nonetheless. Fritz made the introductions: 'This is Mimi and this is Atam. An acquaintance of his gave him the wrong keys, so now he's looking to spend the night at your place.' Atam bowed and explained that he was expecting a spare key to Andrea's apartment to arrive at any time and was therefore, most reluctant to return to his own apartment. 'Are you wanted by the police?' enquired Mimi out of the blue. She held the collar of her bathrobe a little tighter as she did so, twiddling her bright red fingernails.

'Potentially,' replied Atam. 'I know it might sound a little strange, but incidentally I have been an unwitting witness to someone accidentally shooting himself.' 'Oh,' said Mimi with tremendous irony, a tight smile fixed on her puckered lips. 'How sweet. A mysterious man who has witnessed a crime and wants to go into hiding.' She pursed her lips as she held out the hand that had been holding the lapels of her bathrobe tight across her chest. 'Do come in. You're just the sort of person I've been looking for to complete my collection.' She took Atam by the hand and drew him into her apartment. Once Fritz had crossed the threshold too, she nimbly shut the door with her foot.

As Mimi led Atam by the hand through the hallway deeper into the apartment, the driver gave Atam a boisterous shoulder slap from behind. He then furrowed his brow in a manly insinuating way and murmured, 'See? What did I say? You're in!' Mimi guided Atam into the living room and over to the window, drew the curtains aside and turned him towards the evening light some 2900 Kelvin in luminosity, rendering his delicately featured, oval-shaped face vivid and soft and making his fawn-coloured skin glow softly. 'Such dark and mysterious eyes! Like real stars!' chirruped Mimi appreciatively as she turned his face this way and that with both hands, inspecting him at length. As she did so, her bathrobe fell open entirely, revealing somewhat enhanced breasts between slender, athletic shoulders. She immediately let go of Atam's head, laughed pointedly, and with an elf-like gesture pulled the terry cloth bathrobe closed at the lapels with one hand while gracefully giving Atam a feminine slap with the other. 'I'll show you my appendix scar later,' she said without blushing.

This was more than could be said of Atam, who did blush visibly despite his dark complexion as he begged her forgiveness. He thought he had accidentally ruined everything without actually being guilty of anything – but then, little did he know Mimi. She held the back of her hand up towards his face. 'Kiss!' she commanded. With his hopes thus rekindled, he kissed her fingers one after the other for as long as Mimi held out her hand. The scent of soap and her hand cream put him in a rather good mood. 'Respect, Atam!' said Fritz, bursting with admiration. 'You're not in the door for three minutes and already you're allowed to kiss her fingers.' Atam did not answer for fear of saying the wrong thing.

'Isn't he cute?' purred Mimi as she rewarded Atam with a pat on the cheek. The scent of soap along with the hand cream and a hint of nail polish combined with the warmth radiating from her fingertips put him at ease. Still eager to scrutinise Atam further, she opened both halves of the window. The wind toyed with the curtains and Mimi's blonde hair. Meanwhile, Fritz could be heard uncorking a bottle of sparkling wine in the kitchen. Presently, he knocked on the open door of the living room as if to demonstrate some sense of decorum.

Without waiting for an answer, Fritz tiptoed through the living room. The champagne flutes he was holding by the stems in one hand clinked with every step he took. In his other hand, he held the foaming and somewhat overflowing bottle of sparkling wine.

'Well, then, cheers – and here's to new acquaintances,' said Fritz. 'And to love,' he teased as Mimi held her glass out towards Atam, waving Fritz aside with a dismissive gesture. 'I always get so thirsty when I'm excited,' she commented more for her benefit than anyone else's, fidgeting in barely contained anticipation as she waited to clink glasses with Atam. Fritz added his own champagne flute to the other two as they all toasted and subsequently drained their glasses. Fritz refilled them immediately, and this time Atam was eager to beat him to it by raising a toast of his own: 'To Mimi, who really ought to be called Xenia, the goddess of hospitality.' 'Oh, what a sweet talker,' Mimi murmured to Fritz. 'How glad and grateful I am that you have brought him to me.' She toasted Fritz, winking at him with her long false eyelashes before emptying her glass once again and instantly holding it up so it could be refilled.

In the silence that followed all the toasting and drinking, Atam's stomach began to rumble again. Mimi asked whether he was hungry and, after a short pause, whether he would like something sweet to eat. She added that, since he himself was already so sweet, perhaps he only liked savouries. At the mention of the word 'savouries', she turned her face meaningfully towards the evening light and narrowed her eyes to slits, examining him all the better, then clucked her tongue and giggled. Atam apologised for his unruly stomach and explained that he would indeed like something to eat as he had not eaten since noon, may Fritz be his witness. Mimi clapped her hands ebulliently and pondered the matter. All she had left in the refrigerator were leftover fluffy *Buchteln* rolls, but no vanilla sauce as Fritz had licked all the remaining vanilla sauce off her belly earlier that day.

She ordered everyone to walk to the kitchen and see what else was left over as she took Atam by the hand. He was most enthusiastic, explaining that he was in fact a dab hand at rustling up leftovers and asked permission to demonstrate his skills. Mimi squealed with delight at this suggestion, exclaiming, 'I'm not letting this one out of my sight ever again!' In the kitchen, the evening light streaming in across the corridor from the atrium courtyard bathed everything in dim yet colourful lighting, just bright enough to reveal, opposite, a kitchen counter with a white enamelled sink piled high with unwashed dishes. Mimi switched on the light and a fluorescent neon tube above the kitchen counter flickered to life with a yellowish hue. Still holding Atam by the hand, Mimi squatted on her heels in front of the fridge, exposing to the pale light of the open fridge her bare knees that whitened as blood ceased to flow there.

IX

'Delightful!' uttered Atam, which Mimi, cooing with gratitude, naturally inferred was in reference to her legs (the refrigerator was, after all, almost bare and rather dirty). She smiled at Atam meaningfully and got up. 'I'm now going to make myself pretty for you two, and you,' she said, turning to Atam, 'are going to work your magic for us. Fritz will assist you.'

And then Atam asked Fritz to wash and dice some tomatoes and peel some onions. Fritz replied that Atam should not take too literally what Mimi had said about Fritz being seconded to him as a commis chef and that he, Fritz, did have a say in the matter. Atam merely shrugged his shoulders and Fritz did as he was told. He set himself up at the breakfast table by the corridor window, diced the tomatoes and peeled the onions, slicing the latter into disintegrating concentric rings with tear-filled eyes. When the hot-water boiler finally ceased its roaring, Atam became fearful that Mimi might finish prettifying herself sooner than he would be finished with the cooking. After he had folded all the ingredients into the beaten eggs, he allowed the mix to flow smoothly onto the shortcrust pastry in the blue enamelled baking tray, which he had found (and washed) in the sink, and then slid the dish into the oven. Next, he looked for the cutlery and again found it soaking in old dirty water in the sink. He washed it hastily and dried it by shaking off the water droplets.

The light went dim as a hairdryer could be heard exhaling angrily in the bathroom. While they set the rosewood coffee table for dinner, Mimi stepped out of the bathroom. 'No peeking!' she called out as she scurried into another room. They lit the candles, filled the glasses and waited expectantly. Atam's stomach had started rumbling again. After some time, Mimi eventually reappeared in a sleeveless red coat-dress, wearing high-heeled low-cut blue silk pumps. Each time she stepped down hard on her high heels, the curled locks of her shoulder-length hair extended downwards, immediately springing back up again as her knees flexed. She shook her head vigorously to add even more bounce and sway to her hair, stamped her right foot and said, 'Well? What do you think?'

Both gentlemen clapped their hands. 'Oh la la!' they exclaimed. As Fritz wolf-whistled, Mimi stamped her right foot once again and asked how much longer she was supposed to wait for a glass of bubbles. Fritz and Atam immediately handed her their glasses and she took both, sipping from one and then the other, laughing ever so haughtily as if there could be nothing more uplifting in the whole world than her granting them the favour of taking hold of their champagne flutes and helping herself to both.

The oven timer pinged in the kitchen and so, Atam left the small gathering to fetch the dish, a look of mock concentration on his face. 'Mmmh,' said Mimi, relishing the moment. 'That smells delicious. I have to hand it to you, Atam: you really are a keeper.' She pursed her lips and clucked her tongue.

Atam, now praised to the hilt, served up the quiche with assurance and, once everyone had a helping on their plate, went to sit down. But before he could take a seat in the second armchair, Mimi drew him next to her on the couch. She raised her glass and once again they all toasted to each other's health. As Atam brought his glass to his lips, Mimi shook her head with disapproval, a gesture he would come to experience many more times. She hooked her arm under his and they both drank the brotherhood ritual, after which she offered her lips up for a kiss. His lips lingered on her mouth for far too long – then, with a loud clattering tone, his phone suddenly signalled an incoming message. She confiscated his phone without interrupting their kiss and stuffed it under her seat cushion. Fritz's phone then buzzed loudly and he involuntarily read the message. 'It's some other woman,' Mimi explained to Atam, and turning to Fritz, she continued: 'I've told you a thousand times: you're to switch that stupid phone off when you're with me.'

Fritz went on typing on the display as if he had not heard Mimi's instructions. Then the phone underneath Mimi buzzed again and that was the straw that finally broke the camel's back. 'Give me that phone right now,' she ordered, reaching out her hand, 'I sincerely hope you haven't sent your message,' she bellowed, looking sternly into his face. Fritz responded by shaking his head vigorously. She then turned to face Atam and gave him an intense stare as if he had a secret and she was about to expose it. 'You can make us some coffee now,' she suddenly commanded.

Atam carefully brought in the bubbling espresso maker and, without spilling a drop, poured coffee into each of the cups in one fell swoop. He was about to sit down again when Mimi asked where the milk and sugar were. Atam, thanking her, replied that he took his coffee black. Mimi countered that she always took two sugars and a dash of cream. 'And? What about the stirring?' Mimi raised her eyebrows and as she waited for Atam to finish stirring, she unbuttoned a few buttons of her dress right down to the waist. Then, somewhat surprisingly, she threw one leg up into his lap and the other diagonally across to Fritz, pushed aside the folds of her dress that still covered her legs, exposing them all the way up to her panties and pointed to her two garters of different colours. 'Up to here and no further!'

Mimi squealed with delight as Atam ran his fingernails along her shin. Then as he progressed to the back of her knee, she flinched ever so slightly, warning Atam not to tickle her. Atam nodded guiltily. With one hand, he supported Mimi's thigh at her Achilles tendon and with the other, he stroked her leg firmly, cautiously interrupting his gliding movement every few centimetres to massage her calf muscle with his fingertips, all of which Mimi acknowledged several times with moans of pleasure.

But after a while Mimi became even more inattentive as her hips began to hurt from holding her legs out in such an awkward manner. Restlessly, she began shifting her buttocks this way and that. Atam, realising her discomfort, took hold of her leg by the calf with both hands and folded it gently, moving her heel up towards her pelvis as Mimi's eyes widened, a warm smile flitting across her face. She cursorily ran her fingers through his hair and blew him a kiss. 'You really are very sweet,' she said, grabbing him by the hair to pull his face down into her lap. Atam pushed the coffee table aside with his hip to gain more space and massaged her toes. She let her hand linger in his hair and, from time to time, like a bored lioness, nervously ran her hand through it, grabbing his hair time and again to shake his head.

X

The next day, just before noon, Atam woke up crouching on the floor in front of the sofa. He shook Fritz awake. Mimi was nowhere to be seen. He went into the kitchen to make coffee and, while it was brewing, walked around Mimi's apartment. He found her bedroom: the bed was unmade; clothes lay scattered all over the room on the bed and the carpet. He picked up the red dress from the previous night, laid it out carefully on the bed and opened a window to air the room. Dead flies dropped out of the casement, half of them instantly falling onto the floor, wafted by the wind. The other half dropped onto the window sill and, upon landing, scattered in every direction. Those that remained on the sill were pushed aside by the wind or held back by their own weight. Atam found this to-ing and fro-ing strangely captivating, with the constellation of flies changing all the time. Presently, only a handful of desiccated fly corpses were left on the window sill as, on a whim, the wind suddenly ceased, freezing all movement in time.

He went into the bathroom and showered in Mimi's mini-bathtub, which was complete with a seat. Unable to find a clean towel, he dried himself with Mimi's damp bath towel, still scented with the lingering fragrance of her body wash. As he did so, he examined her paraphernalia on the wash basin and opened the mirror cabinet. Never had he seen so many bottles of nail polish and perfume, so many aluminium tubes and apothecary jars all in use at the same time; in a strange way, he admired Mimi. Atam cleaned the mouldy toothpaste-encrusted wash basin for he abhorred having to wash in a dirty sink. He then immediately proceeded to tidy up the entire bathroom. Since he had been unable to go into hiding at Andrea's, he decided he would spend a few days staying at Mimi's place instead.

There were clothes scattered everywhere just as there had been in Mimi's bedroom. Silvery silk panties lay in a puddle in front of the bathtub; stockings drooped down from the syphon under the wash basin; a half-damp camisole top dangled on a rusty folding chair. In the corner behind the door stood a washing machine of Yugoslav manufacture, which boasted chipped enamel and was flecked with rust stains. On top of the machine were various items of laundry including underwear, socks and a red-and-white chequered tea towel.

Atam began by tossing all the laundry he had found in the bathroom into a single large pile. Next, he collected the dirty laundry from the other rooms and threw it onto the rapidly growing pile in the bathroom. With all the dirty laundry now seemingly rounded up, he began sorting through the items of clothing before putting on the first wash. It was then that the apartment doorbell rang. He hurried to the front door and tried to open it but failed. 'Just a moment please,' he called through the door into the corridor. In a loud voice from the living room, Fritz shouted that Mimi must have locked them in and that, in all likelihood, they would not be able to get out before evening. Atam replied that it would take them all day to do the laundry and tidy up anyway and that they would have to leave the vacuuming and window cleaning for tomorrow as there would not be enough hours left in the day.

He sat down at the kitchen table with a coffee and read the messages on his phone. Seemingly, Mimi had written to Andrea to tell her that Atam was now hers and that she would not be giving him back. She was, however, willing to trade him in for Fritz, an arrangement that would no doubt suit Andrea more anyway since he was always going to be close to her, given that he was the Brigadier's driver. Atam was wondering why he was having to read all this when his phone rang.

'Yes?' said Atam in a gravelly voice. 'Atam speaking.' There was silence on the other end, then a gulping sound, like someone forced to swallow hard after shedding many tears in order to make room for even more tears. 'Is that all you have to say?' sobbed Andrea. Atam, ever the gentleman, exclaimed how nice it was to hear her voice. Andrea began with a somewhat restrained, 'Oh, well, you know how it is,' but then immediately proceeded to ramp up her output: 'Here I am, wrenching my guts out trying to build a new life for us, working my backside off for the two of us and giving up my job for you. And then, immediately, and I repeat, IMMEDIATELY, the very next day, I land myself a new job and surrender to some old womaniser for the sake of OUR future – and yes, my dear, this Brigadier certainly knows how to launch a two-pronged attack! And you? YOU? What do you do? You throw yourself at the feet of the first woman you come across and then let her make me such a disgusting offer rather than throttling her with your own bare hands and forcing her to get down on her knees and apologise to me.'

Andrea began to sob bitterly once again. Meanwhile, Fritz had walked into the kitchen and overheard everything, given that Andrea, for all her self-control, was speaking in quite a loud voice. He gave Atam a thumbs up, nodding in appreciation.

'But Andrea,' Atam began. Andrea did not answer, but he could tell from the pause in the sobbing that she would listen, albeit without endorsing this particular *rapporteur*: she would simply lend him her ear, an apparently neutral yet in reality hostile ear, *audiatur et altera pars* merely so she could gather enough evidence with which to condemn him, in all fairness, with his own words. And indeed, Atam began to talk as if his life now depended on it. He explained that because the keys hadn't been the right ones, he had needed somewhere to stay and that Fritz had offered to put him up at a friend's place. 'Oh please,' interjected Andrea matter-of-factly. 'Leave the driver out of all this, will you? Or are you trying to pair us off too, like that Mimi woman did? Worked it all out nicely amongst yourselves, have you?'

Atam protested, adding that Fritz's acquaintance did, after all, live nearby. At this, Andrea sobbed loudly, interrupting him by saying, 'Oh, how convenient, Atam! And just how long were you planning to let this arrangement go on for?' Would he be running back to his Mimi, who conveniently lived just around the corner, whenever she – Andrea – went out to work? She pronounced Mimi's name with contemptuous indifference, as if to withdraw morally from Atam through forced habituation to his incessant and long-standing deceptions. Atam protested. He had, on arrival, immediately been offered some sparkling wine and had not wished to appear rude or reluctant. Atam further pleaded his case, saying his stomach had then started rumbling and in order not to make a fuss or be a nuisance to anyone, he had decided to bake a quiche with the leftovers.

'Oh, so I was right to show the Brigadier ALL my gratitude for the new job and welcome his advances? I felt awful about it. But all YOU have to do is make your stomach rumble just as you made it rumble for me the day before yesterday so I would take care of you. You just make it rumble for any woman who comes along, for a mere glass of sparkling wine,' Andrea countered.

Atam went on to say he had no way of preventing his stomach from rumbling and that even he felt that his rumbling stomach was a truly personal and intimate issue, which was why he had had to get some food immediately and chose to cook for everyone present.

'So you decide to start cooking for a complete stranger and her crony instead of doing everything you can to get hold of the keys to my apartment from Uncle László, who – let's not forget – instantly took you into his family, and then pack my things and hand them over to my employer's driver for immediate delivery to me so I can sleep in my own pyjamas and not have to accept a man's shirt from Herr Brigadier to cover my nakedness whenever I go to the bathroom via the barracks corridor,' interjected Andrea with faultless objectivity.

'But Andrea, you were the one who hung up on me and told me to wait until you got back in touch,' Atam countered.

'And yet, Atam, when it comes to your Mimi, you don't wait for her to get in touch either: you just follow her right there and then,' retorted Andrea, putting the ball back in his court.

'She's not MY Mimi, Andrea,' Atam replied. 'The driver…'

'Fritz,' Andrea interrupted. 'You can say "Fritz", you know; I'll be using that name myself soon enough.'

'Well, the driver got a call right in the middle of dinner and that was when she became furious and confiscated both our phones and hid them under her seat cushion.'

'Oh, so now we're talking about her backside as well, are we? God, the things I have to listen to. And anyway, what do I care about Fritz's phone? What do you say to that?' Andrea hissed.

'Then, after dinner, I made coffee,' Atam continued regardless. 'Because by then she was already so tipsy she was getting more and more obnoxious and pushy, but as always I behaved like a gentleman.'

'Except it doesn't look like it did you any good because, from what I've just read, you're now hers!' Andrea commented forcefully.

'With the coffee she asked us to massage her legs, and every time we made a wrong movement she scolded us,' said Atam unrelentingly.

'Well, at least that's something the Brigadier knows how to do. Maybe he can show you sometime,' countered Andrea.

'And now we're both locked up inside her apartment and I'm cleaning the flat because I can't stand this mess. Plus, I suppose I'm going to have to stay here until I get your key.'

'Well congratulations! All the best!' And with that she hung up. She did not pick up again whenever Atam tried calling her time and time again later on.

Atam vacuumed the living room. The chrome-plated suction pipe rumbled and crackled wherever Atam happened to move the vacuum brush across the carpet. He began to worry he might get some foreign object or other stuck in the soles of his bare feet. And how often had he regretted affording space to some unfortunate and unhappy thought, thereby creating a crystallisation point in reality. Indeed, fears and apprehensions are often nothing other than the beginnings of real processes merely glimpsed out of the corner of one's eye that could just about be avoided simply by looking away.

Time and again his thoughts returned to Andrea, and time and again he consoled himself about Andrea's scolding with thoughts of Mimi. For even if Mimi gave him little or no credit for cleaning up her apartment and scolded him into the bargain, there was far more warmth and teasing in Mimi's emotional outbursts than in Andrea's bizarre accusations and her dead-eyed seriousness.

Atam ran the vacuum brush along the edge of the Persian rug before bisecting the carpet area with a diagonal sweep. He first cleaned one of the triangles thus formed and just as he was about to focus on the second, he stepped on a shard of glass. He cried out, more in fright than in pain, and threw himself onto the sofa, his foot bleeding. He raised his leg as droplets of blood trickled from the wound on his big toe onto the orange table-runner on the coffee table. He tried to see what was sticking into his toe but could not see anything from that angle while looking down, so he asked Fritz to take a look. Without hesitation, Fritz pulled out a sizable shard of champagne flute, thereby causing blood to gush from the wound. He immediately pressed the open wound shut with his thumb and waited for the bleeding to stop. 'You're not going to be able to clean up Mimi's flat like that now.'

Fritz went in search of bandages and returned with a pair of nail scissors, some eau de Cologne and a very small pair of women's knickers. He cut the underwear into square patches and dabbed the wound clean with the fragrant plasters, leaving it to dry in the air. After this, they both stretched out in the armchairs to take a well-earned rest.

XI

During her short lunch break, Mimi had hurried to buy groceries for her prisoners and was carrying them home as fast as her sore feet would allow after four hours of standing in high heels. As there was no one waiting for her in the hallway to take the groceries off her, she carried them into the kitchen herself where, in addition to the all-too-familiar tower of unwashed dishes in the kitchen sink, she encountered even smaller and more recent stacks of dirty dishes on the draining board.

Somewhat disgruntled, she made her way to the bathroom to wash her hands, stepping over a large pile of laundry in the process to get to the wash basin. As there was no dry towel to hand, she stormed into the living room in a foul mood, her fingers still dripping wet.

Clapping her hands loudly and stamping her feet, she yelled at them, asking whether they were completely out of their minds to trash her apartment that way while she had gone off to work. There she was working her backside off while they indulged in bloody orgies on her carpet and shredded her underwear to bits. Atam, still groggy from his morning nap, made several clumsy attempts to get up even though he had been caught off-guard and confessed that it was all his fault and that Fritz had only tried to help him in order to prevent the worst.

Mimi, now feigning an air of sympathetic understanding, wrung her hands and, in a motherly and somewhat condescending tone, exclaimed with apparent concern that good old Atam was bravely shouldering all the blame but that it would do him no good since he now belonged to her anyway. Even without his magnanimous confession, she would bring the full force of her wrath to bear down on him, and he would soon find himself simpering and begging for her to be nice to him once again. But it would be to no avail, no avail at all; in fact, to make her point, Mimi escalated the situation even further by ordering Atam to hurry into the kitchen that instant and cook them lunch as she had to be back at work in half an hour and earn a livelihood since, quite evidently, these men were good for nothing anyway.

After that, Atam would be required, first of all, to clean up the mess in the bathroom, do the laundry, the ironing and then put everything away in the wardrobes. Fritz, for his part, was told to leave and amuse himself for an entire evening for a change to see what that was like for him. And after all this upset and all these worries, she really did need an evening to herself for once and Atam should hopefully realise that it was up to him to make sure she enjoyed a nice evening in order to win back her trust and affections. Atam noticed that by the end of her rant, Mimi's tone had become rather more conciliatory. Keen not to give her any reason to depart from it once again, he headed off to the kitchen and, as he walked past, bent down low to Mimi's hand and fleetingly kissed her moist fingertips.

Meanwhile, Fritz had recorded the entire scene on his phone and was in the process of sending the video clip to Atam's phone when he suddenly attracted Mimi's attention. She asked what he was doing. 'Nothing,' Fritz replied, explaining that he had just recorded the scene. With the hand that Atam had just kissed, she hinted at an imminent slap and demanded that the recording be deleted immediately. Fritz pretended to obey and fiddled around with his device, which appeared to calm Mimi down a little. Just as she had the previous day, she sat down on the sofa and threw her legs up onto Fritz's lap in a rather unladylike way so he could remove her high heels and massage her toes.

Atam found several bottles of sparkling wine in the fridge that were still warm to the touch, and two crowns of Extrawurst sausage. On the kitchen countertop was a net of potatoes already sprouting young shoots, a few carrots, a white cabbage, and a head of wilted lettuce. Finding none of it particularly inspiring, he was nonetheless reduced once again to cooking with whatever there was.

As he took the Extrawurst out of the fridge and put a saucepan of water on to boil, he resolved that tomorrow, he really would have to convince Mimi to let him out of the house so he himself could go shopping. He rinsed the wilted lettuce and let it sit for a moment to crisp up. Next, he rounded up the crockery he needed and washed it in the sink. He made a warm sausage salad with onions on green lettuce by way of a decorative base.

Mimi stared at this menu du jour in bafflement and, as Atam returned with three glasses of water, inquired as to the meaning of such a disgusting concoction? Did he really think she could eat onions on her lunch break? Had he perhaps mistaken her for a ploughman? She reminded him she worked as a sales assistant in an organic vegan food store and had to be able to converse with her customers in a cultivated way without them keeling over or breaking out in a rash. Was he incapable of cooking anything better than pork sausages? Yesterday he had boasted that he could cook the most delicious meals out of leftovers and yet today, after she had sacrificed her lunch break to buy groceries, he could think of nothing more imaginative than boiling a sausage? She might as well have gone straight to the sausage stand and saved herself the trouble of shlepping groceries around in her high heels. Plus, she would have been spared the whole calamitous situation she had just encountered at home. She then threw her hands up in horror, invoked the Almighty and began sobbing bitterly.

Atam kneeled down in front of Mimi and started to massage her knee. Once again, he used his hip to nudge the coffee table aside and lay his face on Mimi's lap, caressing the small of her back, and then slid lower and grabbed both her buttocks. Mimi smiled contentedly. 'At last, you're getting something right, my little Atam,' she said and pushed her hips closer to Atam and pressed his head against her lap with both hands, so much so that he could barely breathe.

After a few minutes, she let him go and patted her thighs energetically and then got to her feet as if keen to re-join the troops on the front line. 'Right, I'm off.' Atam escorted Mimi to the door. In the hallway, he asked her whether she might allow him out so he could go shopping. 'Can I trust you?' asked Mimi in return, her eyes wide with inquiry. She answered her question herself: 'Tomorrow maybe; you've got enough on your hands here today. Get Fritz to give you my telephone number and you can write me a short shopping list.'

And with that she stepped out into the corridor and began hesitantly to close the door shut behind her, peeking yearningly at Atam's face through the narrowing gap. Then, with a giggle, she slammed the door fully shut and locked it. Atam heard the receding sound of her heels clacking hard on the Solnhofen flagstones that paved the hallways and corridors of the entire Gründerzeit building.

He walked back into the apartment and put on a very hot wash to disinfect the machine. He then gathered up the lunch from the living room and emptied the food into the rubbish bin, except for one piece of sausage, which, as his stomach growled yet again, he hastily grabbed a bite of it right there and then. Next, he washed all the dishes and stacked them up on top of the dishtowels he had laid out on the draining board. After he had finished, he went to the bathroom to empty out the washing machine and then carried the clean bedding into the bedroom and hung it up on a clothes dryer in front of the window.

Back in the living room, Atam finally got round to picking up all the makeshift bandaging and asked Fritz to put a large plaster on his cut. He went back to the kitchen, put on his socks and washed the kitchen floor. While it was drying, he granted himself a short break and made coffee for Fritz and himself. He served it in the living room, threw himself down on Mimi's seat on the sofa and asked Fritz whether there was any news. Fritz replied that earlier on, he had accidentally sent the video recording of Mimi's little outburst not to Atam's phone, as intended, but to Andrea's. This was because her number had been the one last stored on the app, which he had failed to notice, what with Mimi breathing down his neck the whole time. He had desperately been searching for it ever since on all the data processing systems in the world, trying to retract and delete the message retrospectively. 'Oh, for goodness' sake,' Atam snapped. 'I wish I'd never asked.'

At that moment, Atam's phone rang and Andrea's number was displayed on the screen. He took the call but Andrea remained silent. Atam spoke to say that he was really happy to hear from her. She responded by asking whether he enjoyed poking fun at her, given that she had deliberately remained silent to give Atam a chance to explain himself. But then she added that what she had just seen on her phone was so unbelievable that there could really be no explanation.

'But Andrea,' Atam began. 'You must have seen I was injured and what a scene Mimi was creating?' Andrea went on: 'All I saw was a disappointed woman coming home from work exhausted to find that her apartment, which she had arranged and furnished with much love and attention, had been trashed by you. And I thought to myself how lucky I was to have given you the wrong key and that you had not had the opportunity to make a mess of my apartment as well, which I would have opened up to you willingly and lovingly, just as Uncle László had lovingly taken you into my family and still you ignored him and preferred to go to some strange woman's place. All I can say, once again, is that I wish you all the best.'

Andrea hung up before Atam could put his case. The fact that she had called him once again told him that she did want something from him or was at least planning something with him. Otherwise, why would she, who had after all landed herself a fine catch in the shape of the Brigadier, keep chasing after him all the time and scolding him into the bargain? But what could she possibly want from him? And, even more interestingly, what could she possibly want from the peculiar Brigadier himself?

But there was no time to ponder these thoughts further; after all, Mimi might soon be home and the housework really ought to be done by then. And hence, Atam took Fritz's coffee cup off him, went into the kitchen, washed it and placed it on top of the towering pile of clean dishes. From the kitchen, he went back to the bathroom and put on the next wash. Then he sat back down in Mimi's place on the sofa to write out his shopping list for her. He began without any particular form of address as he could not think of an adequate form by which to address Mimi. He did not want to appear cold nor did he want to seem overly possessive; after all, they had not yet slept together. But how should he sign off?

No sooner had he sent off his list than his phone rang: it was Mimi. Was he out of his mind? Did he seriously think she could pick up a clothes dryer on her way home? Perhaps he thought a clothes dryer might fit snugly into her counterfeit Prada? She would get him some washing-up liquid, some bread rolls and perhaps even croissants, if he allowed it. Indeed, she herself had a preference for croissants for breakfast, some cold cuts if they still looked appetising come the evening, and anything else that sprang to mind as she walked down the supermarket aisles. Mimi was also keen to know why he thought he needed such a weak light bulb.

So he could read in bed without disturbing her, replied Atam. At this, Mimi laughed pointedly and went on to explain that Atam would have other things to do in bed with her and that he would sleep when she slept, so the problem would not even arise. She laughed brightly once again and told Atam he was so cute. She added that she would be home in twenty minutes and quickly chirruped him a kiss as she hung up.

XII

Atam hurried into the bedroom and began ironing for all he was worth. He ran the iron over each button facing only once. His main thought was to get finished. Next, he put fresh bed linen and sheets on the bed. He took the liberty of adding a duvet cover for himself and two pillows. He made the double-bed look inviting by turning the duvets down on either side in a neat triangular fold.

That was when he heard Mimi's footsteps out in the corridor, and a warm glow filled his chest as she turned her key in the lock. He pulled the door open for her invitingly and courteously stepped back. Mimi entered, brandishing the bag of groceries in front of her before handing it over to Atam. She then quickly slammed the door shut behind her, locked it and removed the key. Atam carried the shopping bag into the kitchen and put it down on the breakfast table next to the corridor window with the coloured panes.

Mimi followed with the inevitable clacking of her high heels. With every step she took, a jolt went through her entire body, lending her movement a rather tantalising touch, something she was well aware of and deliberately chose to do.

In those rare moments when it did slip her mind, it appeared all the more graceful. And so, it was gracefully and tantalisingly that she walked through the kitchen, nodding approvingly and running her index finger along the worktop as she passed. With a degree of satisfaction, she mustered her clean fingertip, nodded yet again and then pulled a face and pursed her lips. She wore her dyed blonde hair tied back in a ponytail with a rubber band with the ends teased out. The shorter hair that was not quite long enough to reach the rubber band fluffed out at the sides. She frowned good-humouredly but left the kitchen without a word, eager not to appear overly friendly.

She opened the door from the hallway into the bathroom just wide enough to peek inside, switched on the light and surveyed the overall cleanliness and tidiness with satisfaction. Then she went into the living room, caught sight of Fritz and, with her index finger, made it clear to him that he was dismissed. Walking ahead of him, she accompanied him to the apartment door and let him out. She returned to the kitchen and then held her foot out to Atam invitingly. By now, he had learnt what such a gesture signified and entailed, here, in Vienna.

Indeed, it was quite different from the rituals at the court of his grandmother, Maharani Sumitra Devi Kandari, the Queen of Jaipur, where *pranama* was the customary reverential form of greeting. There the people granted an audience were required to prostrate themselves in front of her feet and allowed to touch her in order to be suffused with her Majesty's sacred energy and wisdom.

Atam, for his part, squatted down in front of Mimi, placed her foot in his lap and slipped off her ballerina shoe.

He did the same with her other foot and then stood up again without stepping back so as to remain in front of her at close quarters. Mimi held out her cheek, her outstretched index finger pointing to the precise spot where he was to touch her with his lips, and Atam obliged. He then carried her shoes into the hallway and heard Mimi calling after him to draw her a bath and pour her out some fizz. Atam duly prepared the bath and then brought her a glass of sparkling wine.

Mimi sat by the breakfast table and smiled at him. 'You and I are going to get along just fine, Atam,' said Mimi. 'Don't you think?' Atam squatted in front of her, picked up her right foot and massaged her toes and the sole of her foot. 'That's perfect,' Mimi said, leaning back. 'You've no idea how exhausting it was in the shop today. Three women in a row wanted to buy the same *Waldviertel* tofu black pudding that doesn't exist. And the whole time, some snotty-nosed brat was coughing his lungs out in a pram, spluttering all over the deli counter. I was convinced I would come down with the flu. Atam placed her other foot in his lap. Mimi sighed contentedly and stroked Atam's hair. Then, all of a sudden, she stood up and demanded that Atam carry her into the bathroom and undress her.

Atam was not amused. This was not how he had imagined his first intimate evening in Mimi's company. Still, he picked Mimi up in his arms as requested, but he carried her matter-of-factly, the way a hospital orderly might carry a sick patient. 'Watch my head!' she admonished him as they passed through the bathroom door. Atam set her down and was about to leave the bathroom when Mimi grabbed him, forcibly turned his head back towards her and ordered him to close his eyes and undress her.

He closed his eyes and felt his way along her neck to her blouse, moving along its collar until he sensed her throat. He then reached for the top button, undid it and slid his fingers lower to undo the next button as well, the back of his hand feeling the incipient curve of her breasts. As he undid the next button, his hand was now immersed between Mimi's warm breasts and he could feel her satin skin, soft against his hand. But suddenly he heard and felt a slap strike him resoundingly in the middle of his face, leaving a burning sensation on his cheek. He could hear Mimi shouting at him and asking what he thought he was playing at, closing his eyes when he undressed her, as if there was a man alive who would not be willing to have his eyes gouged out just for the opportunity to catch sight of her breasts. Sobbing dramatically, she pushed Atam back and dashed behind the shower curtain into the bath. Atam was surprised. He should have known that Mimi would play him for a fool.

He went back into the kitchen to fetch her a glass of sparkling wine. Mimi hissed at him through the door that he was now adding insult to injury by knocking on the door rather than just walking straight in. As Atam entered, she hurled a bar of soap and a sponge at him. The champagne glass took a direct hit, fell from his hand and shattered on the tiled floor. Mimi, still holding the shower curtain aside, was now visible as she stood naked in the tub, hot water running over her steaming body. Right then Atam had no desire whatsoever to feast his eyes on her. Besides, he had the broken glass to clean up. Mimi shook her head. More tears were now running down her cheeks.

A little while later, she went barefoot in her kimono to find Atam in the kitchen. He handed Mimi his glass of sparkling wine and complimented her, saying she was the most beautiful woman he had ever seen. Mimi was forced to laugh and she corrected Atam, saying that she was in fact the most beautiful woman Atam had ever *not* seen. They both laughed rather sheepishly, and Mimi accepted the glass from his hand just as she had the day before without holding her kimono shut. As the garment opened up, she watched Atam's eyes with keen interest as they scrutinised her. She allowed herself to be studied and admired at length. Then she laughed once again, ordered Atam to bring her some more sparkling wine and headed straight for the living room. There she sat down on the sofa in a most ladylike fashion before deciding to lie on her back so she could stretch her legs out and bicycle the air with them.

Mimi emptied the glass in one long gulp without setting it down. She then wiped her lips with the back of her hand and called out loudly into the kitchen: 'More!' And so, it continued in this vein for a while until the first bottle was empty. Mimi stretched out on the sofa, humming an old pop song to herself while making seductive eyes at him.

Now back in the kitchen, Atam cooked and tasted, blanched and peeled, grated nuts, steamed noodles, rinsed the lettuce and arranged the dinner on the largest plates he could find in the pile of dishes he had washed that afternoon. He lit two new candles and carried them ceremoniously into the living room. Mimi was all curled up on the sofa, sucking her thumb and snoring rather fetchingly.

XIII

He woke up to Mimi's head resting on his upper arm. He pushed her hair away from her face and tucked it behind her ears, thereby waking her up. She turned away from him energetically, put on a grumpy face and, with an irritated tone, asked what the time was and what he thought he was playing at. Atam replied that he had no idea what the time was and that he merely wanted to wish her a good morning. Mimi retorted that there was no way this was a good morning. She was now going to be late for work and would have to go out without breakfast and, more importantly, coffee – all of which was entirely Atam's fault. She doubled down, stating that Atam was in fact simply good for nothing, nothing at all.

Mimi got out of bed, slipped on her bathrobe and, with a naturally graceful gesture, brushed the hair out of her face, all the while intimating to Atam, unrelentingly, just how little she thought of him. Not only had he been incapable of serving her dinner on time and then satisfying her in bed, but he had also not at all behaved in a manner befitting a gentleman, showing not even a quantum of responsibility by waking her up on time that very morning so she could go to work and earn a living. Indeed, he had had nothing else in mind, no other ambition in life than to loiter about her apartment all day and turn the place upside down.

Atam too got up and went into the kitchen – unclothed – to make breakfast so Mimi could at least wash down a couple of bites with some coffee before she hurried away. She did not take long in the bathroom and by the time she walked into the kitchen, the coffee was hissing its way up inside the espresso maker. She walked past Atam, instructing him to go and put on some clothes: did he think they were living in some sort of alpine hut? She grabbed a glass from the bottom of the pile of dried dishes, which caused part of the stratified structure to collapse with a crash, leading her to mutter, 'That's all I needed!' as she poured water into her glass. From a drawer next to the sink, she took out a packet of Alka-Seltzer and attempted, awkwardly and with delayed gratification, to eject a tablet from its plastic strip using only one hand. She scolded Atam in the process for not even being able to get her a headache tablet from the packet. Evidently, he preferred to stand around in an utterly useless way, worshipping the coffeemaker, without a thought for her. She popped the tablet into her mouth and took big gulps from the water glass, much in the same way she had from the champagne glass the previous day, and the day before that.

By now the coffee was ready, and Atam poured a bowl of coffee half-full for Mimi and fetched the milk bottle from the refrigerator, placing it next to the coffee cup on the breakfast table. He then stepped away to head towards the bathroom and was about to leave the kitchen when Mimi snapped at him once again, chiding him for acting like a typical male yet again and thinking only of himself, leaving her to fetch her own sugar in the bargain. She added that it was obvious for all to see that Atam was not in the least interested in her. Had it not been so, he would have thought of these elementary little things himself, but clearly, he did not care about her in the slightest.

Atam turned around again and was about to take two sugar lumps from the sugar bowl next to the steaming coffee cup and drop them into Mimi's cup when she angrily enquired whether he was now planning to show off his dangling manhood to the whole building on Gilgegasse; after all, someone she knew could come along and walk past at any moment. Had he ever in his entire life pursued anything else other than his own self-interest and assumed responsibility for anything?

Atam went off to the bathroom. Mimi shouted after him, rather sarcastically, asking who was supposed to stir her coffee now. He got washed and dressed. By the time he walked back into the corridor, Mimi was standing there in her bathrobe, the belt knotted around her waist. While brushing her hair, she opened the apartment door for him and stared right past him rather cuttingly. Seeing him hesitate, she enquired whether he needed a written permission to leave and if so, would he like her to read it out loud to him as well. In a flash he skipped past her rather cockily and, without glancing behind him, clicked his heels together in a joyful leap.

As he stepped out of the building onto the street, he was blinded by the glare of the sun. He pulled his phone out of his jacket pocket and called Gretchen; after all, he now had to find someplace else to stay. It took Gretchen a long time to pick up, and when she did, she was somewhat out of breath.

'The first thing I want you to do is activate your phone tracking; I almost died not knowing where the photos were. What were you thinking, not getting in touch for two whole days? And who is supposed to look after me in the meantime? Have you no heart? Where are you anyway?'

'I'd rather not say in case you're being bugged. But I do have the photos with me. I went into hiding at a new acquaintance's place, but she has just turfed me out.'

'Well, I'm afraid you can't come to my place right now either,' said Gretchen, giggling. 'I have a gentleman friend visiting.'

'I thought I was supposed to console you?'

'Someone else is attending to that right now. If I hung around waiting for you, I'd be forever unhappy and alone. So, I've reheated the old Kosteletzky.'

'My condolences.'

'Well, I'm not jumping with joy either. You'll have to console me for having to let the likes of him console me. It's all your fault anyway!'

'Why don't you get rid of him and I'll come to your place?'

'Thank you, you're too kind, but that would be quite rude. I'll hurry up and finish off what I'm doing here and get back to you.'

As Gretchen blew him a kiss through the phone, Atam crossed Alserstrasse and hurried over to the waiting bus. He sat down near the rear exit, far away from the driver. This time the wooden seat vibrated excitedly under the impetus of the engine. At Lerchenfelderstrasse, he alighted, and on a whim, decided to walk downhill to Neudeggergasse rather than turn straight into Piaristengasse.

From Lerchenfelderstrasse, he could hear music coming from a loudspeaker van that was slowly crawling up the slight incline from Palais Auersberg as he strode down Neudeggergasse away from Lerchenfelderstrasse. His curiosity piqued; he slowed his steps to give the vehicle a chance to catch up with him. A constant hissing and growling issued forth from the loudspeakers. He soon spotted the vehicle turning into Neudeggergasse and approaching him. The thought briefly entered his mind that Mimi or Andrea might be inside the vehicle, or indeed they might both have joined forces as a result of Fritz's intercession. He did, however, have to concede that this last thought might be rather too far-fetched as Fritz would never do such a dastardly thing. In any case, he remained rooted to the spot so he could listen to the broadcast.

A brisk march-like chant could be heard, gradually deconstructed by the echoes reverberating off the walls of the surrounding buildings, all the while erratically amplified. The polyphonic chorus began to blur somewhat as the guitar accompaniment bounced ever more harshly off the façades, resonating roughly down Neudeggergasse, which was deserted apart from him. Atam began to walk further down Neudeggergasse. With a slow and measured pace so as not to attract undue attention or arouse suspicion that he might be about to make a run for it, he put one foot in front of the other, as if without intent. He then came to a halt and took to observing, comparing and even contrasting the variations in the embellishments on the Gründerzeit façades around him: while repetitive in structure they were nonetheless different in detail. Just then a deep-purple vocal took over the lead, amplifying with Andrea-like intensity into brief coloraturas pitched on the word 'through', with the 'r' emphatically rolled with Mimiesque rhoticity.

Atam decided to quicken his step to see whether the loudspeaker van would also track him more quickly, which would in any case be suspicious and entitle him to respond or, at the very least, turn around, look at the van and reconnoitre who might be at the wheel. And indeed, the vehicle did pick up speed as Atam hurried along. It was, however, far too conspicuous and linear to be suspicious. No pursuer tailing him would match his walking pace so blatantly, if only not to alert him.

And so, Atam walked on. Eager to spring a trap on the driver of the vehicle, he turned downhill into Josefgasse, against the one-way street, and crossed in front of Vienna's English Theatre, pretending to be engrossed in the display window of the firearms shop with its array of wellington boots and cookbooks. But in reality, he was watching the loudspeaker van in the reflection of the window, and when he saw the van turn into the street against the one-way system, he realised instantly that Mimi or Andrea, or both, had to be inside the vehicle and hence, he opted to enter the shop premises.

XIV

Atam was greeted with much deferential bowing, and no explanations or brandishing of IDs were required of him as he curtly expressed his desire to go down to the shooting range. Rather, the door promptly and noiselessly sprang open for him and he made his way down the staircase to the basement premises below.

A heavy, amply padded iron door opened electrically, swaying to a halt half-ajar. Atam stepped into the anteroom of the shooting gallery. He was greeted once again by the manager in charge of the digital cinema, his eyes now discreetly lowered. Atam was asked which programme he wished to watch in the digital shooting cinema. 'Duel,' replied Atam without hesitation. He stepped into the auditorium draped in white cloth. As he waited for his own personal pistol – it had been at the gunsmith's for servicing – and two magazines packed with 9 mm high velocity full metal jacket cartridges to be brought to him, he slipped into his electric vest and connected the XLR plug to the console. The projector cast a test-card image onto the paper screen with a bulletproof trap set up behind it. 'Right, so, for the backdrop, a forest clearing in the Prater and, halfway down the tunnel, I want the *Portrait of An Unknown Woman* by Ivan Kramskoy, seated in her open carriage, as the onlooker. Opposite me, in the centre of the field, if you please, my adversary in a red tailcoat, beige waistcoat and green top-hat.'

Satisfied, he tested the weight of the nickel-plated Browning Hi-Power in his hand, relishing its cool, heavy feel. He checked the topmost cartridge with his fingertips, inserted the magazine and raised the loaded gun up to face height, first placing his forehead on it before kissing the middle of the pistol slide, sparing a thought for and silently thanking John Moses Browning. The first moving image featured a secluded clearing near the Mauthnerwasser canal at dawn, and he popped in his tactical earplugs. Atam felt that there was something tremendously exciting about the *Unknown Woman*, with her confident gaze and contemptuously lascivious, but by no means mean, mouth that showed barely a flicker of emotion, blending simply – and perhaps a touch nervously – with the rest of her face as she observed the proceedings. What an exciting prospect to be able to shoot for this lady without the expectation of anything from her in return, Atam thought, pondering whom Kramskoy had actually painted: was she a daughter of the people who had married a nobleman and needed to be alone with herself from time to time in order to recover from the necessary societal adjustments and the continual play-acting? Someone who therefore observed everything with a great deal of earnestness so as to adapt her deportment accordingly? Someone who was so utterly unapproachable and unattainable, even if she found it impossible at any moment to conceal her obvious charms, and knew it? Once Atam's adversary had taken up position, backlit and somewhat unfairly exposing as little of himself as possible (these AI programs could already do all that; in that respect they were extremely human), the random generator decided who was to have the first shot. Atam stood face on and waited for his rival to pull the trigger. A loud bang sounded from the loudspeaker, and Atam felt a light impact on his right arm. He quickly slipped his Browning over to his left hand, pulled the slide through and took aim a hand's width higher than his head. He then slowly lowered his arm and, sweeping his forehead, fired once. His rival fell to the ground, a bullet hole peering between his eyes.

Then, suddenly, the lights of the shooting auditorium came on, a foghorn sounded, and the cinema manager entered the range. Two women of slender build were waiting in the doorway behind him. Both wore a sort of dark grey uniform of stretch trousers and boleros over knitted jumpers and pink trainers; they both stood there, wide-eyed. The cinema manager first apologised to Atam for disturbing him and proceeded to inform him that there were two ladies wishing to speak to him as a matter of urgency. Atam, still holding in his left shooting hand the pistol only slightly warm from the single shot fired, turned away, aimed at the bottom of the dark screen, released the magazine, pulled the slide right back, and caught the cartridge ejected from the chamber. He then tucked his weaponry into his jacket pockets and signalled to the two women to come over.

The taller one of the two wore her long brunette hair in a messy bun, tufts of hair sprouting wildly. The sheen of gossamer hair at her temples and neck gave her an appearance of relaxed tiredness. The shorter one sported an ash-blond Vidal Sassoon five-point cut bob and, as she came to a halt in front of Atam, it swung forward like a hinged helmet suspended loosely from the top of her skull, exploding briefly into individual strands before regrouping and converging into its helmet shape as the hair settled.

He looked at the women's faces in turn; the shorter one seemed to mistake him for someone else, for she looked up at him adoringly. The other, however, was most fidgety, restlessly shifting her weight from one leg to the other, so much so that Atam was about to ask if she was in urgent need of the restroom. Finally, she spoke: 'Where are the restrooms? Down there?' The cinema manager nodded, adding, 'Follow me, please.'

'You are the chosen one,' the blonde now declared. Atam firmly refuted the allegation. 'I'm sorry, sir,' the woman continued forcefully, saying, 'It's not a matter of whether or not you know. The signs have told us so. You were the only one standing in the bright glare of the sun on Neudeggergasse, and so, you have been elected to help save the Earth with us.' No wonder Atam's stomach began to rumble: after all, he had had no breakfast and had already been subjected to an expulsion as well as an escape. He therefore enquired whether they might like to discuss the matter further over breakfast at his apartment.

Back out on the street, Atam took the lead. The two women initially fell into step behind Atam, whispering quietly to themselves. They came to a halt in front of his building on Piaristengasse as he began to search in vain for his keys inside his trouser pocket. Fortunately, the door of the wine shop next to the main gate was wide open, so Atam guided his visitors right through the retail premises into the belly of the building, exiting at the very back through an inconspicuous door leading straight into the stairwell. They climbed up the stairs to the second floor of the late Biedermeier-style building. At his apartment door, Atam chuckled sheepishly, then reached up along the casing of the doorjamb, feeling for his spare key.

He unlocked the front door, excused himself and went into the kitchen to make coffee. The blonde entered the living room alone and sat down in an armchair while the taller one followed him into the kitchen to give him a hand, or so she claimed. With the two of them preparing breakfast, it was ready in no time at all. The woman proved extremely capable and quickly found her way around the unknown household, without the need for any instructions.

Snow White, still seated, introduced herself with a smile, then turned to face Bluebell, promptly eliciting a smile from her too. Atam broke the smile-filled silence a moment later, eager to ask what the two of them actually wanted from him. 'Well then,' said Snow White, smiling all the while as Bluebell too continued to smile, 'My half-sister Bluebell from Chicago' – at this, Bluebell's smile broadened further still – 'and I have ascertained that humankind is destroying the planet. Sheer selfishness has taken hold. It is the reason we are all going to perish and take the entire planet down with us.'

XV

Snow White paused and scrutinised Atam's face to see what effect her words had had on him. Atam seized the opportunity to ask whether in her view, humanity was the Earth's soul. Thrilled by Atam's question, Snow White went on to say that she thought that he was wonderful and that he had immediately grasped the crucial question. 'Well done, Atam; you certainly rule!' Snow White became fidgety with excitement in her chair, clapping her hands as Atam poured her some more cold coffee: 'I'm really amazed at how quickly you grasped the gist of it all after just a few words.' But then she calmed down again, and in a more serious vein, added, 'But alas, no, we are not the soul of the Earth!'

Atam failed to suppress a rather inappropriate smile. He raised his hands somewhat defensively and enquired whether, in that case, humanity was perhaps Earth's defective brain, overlaid across the planet like a cerebral biofilm and somehow in conflict with the instructions from the cosmos and Earth's very core. But Snow White was unperturbed and stated that the duality between the Earth and humanity was indissoluble. She stamped her foot so energetically that the coffee cups began to tremble, sending wavelets of cold coffee to break ashore against the rims of the cups, forming new eruptions of bubbles in the milky skin. She added that only the entity as a whole could ever be saved and that the salvation had to come causally from humanity and would, in any case, also require a direct influence on the Earth.

Atam nodded kindly, smiling engagingly as Snow White's eyes began to widen. He asked what form those influences might take, and Snow White's smile vanished. 'First of all,' she continued sternly, 'we need to reach out to people and make them understand the urgency and, at the same time, ask the Earth to be patient. This, we can best achieve through spiritual Actionism. For example, we will baptise the good people and tattoo our mark of peace on their foreheads, but we will drown the bad people for if we are to succeed, we must break the habit of feeling compassion.'

Atam noticed that a slight redness was flushing the skin of Snow White's face and felt himself rather taken by her enthusiasm. She would turn her head suddenly to the side and hold it there without shaking or jerking so that different strands of hair would fall forward onto her flushed face or sweep across her freckled nose, entangling themselves on her long pale lashes. Atam found it all greatly appealing, and he felt an urge to seduce her.

'Yes,' said Atam, interrupting Snow White. 'That's all wonderful. But who decides what is good or evil?' 'It's very simple,' said Snow White. 'We, as women, feel it in our gut. Our hearts tell us the truth. For thousands of years, we have known this, and for thousands of years, we have been pushed aside because of it – all because the powerful are afraid of the truth. Every woman has a direct connection with infinity in its living manifestation. We shall convene tribunals of women and hold court over all humans.'

By now, almost enraptured, Snow White continued: 'But the most beautiful part will be when we demonstrate through our artistry that we are sixty per cent water and made of stardust. At the opera house, rather than nipping out to eat a Bratwurst at the buffet kiosk during the interval, we will set up inflatable paddling pools and fill them with water before baptising one another naked.' At this point, a thought flashed through Atam's mind as he wondered whether the bad people were also to be drowned in the opera's intermission foyers; he pondered how he might phrase such a question without causing offence.

But Snow White was already elaborating: 'We will use thermal cameras to capture the images of our blood flowing inside our bodies and project it onto large screens that we will suspend there and then from the cornices and column capitals. We will render visible through ultrasound the pulsating beat within us and project it onto the screens. And during the recording, we will sip water and show it cascading inside us, spreading and filling us up.'

Snow White gave Atam a quizzical look; he, for his part, had been waiting for such a propitious moment. Nodding in agreement, he raised his brow, wide-eyed, and opined that it all sounded rather wonderful and that he thought it was great. Snow White appeared relieved; her eyes became even larger and a smile swelled her cheeks.

Bluebell now asked Atam for some coffee as he had been entirely engrossed in Snow White and had, in the process, neglected his duties as host. Snow White in turn raised her eyebrows coquettishly, being confident of victory.

As reluctant as he was to jeopardise the good mood that had now established itself, he had to ask questions, if only to show interest. So he asked her how many people were now in the movement, who owned the car with the loudspeaker, and by what means the ultrasound probes, printed forms, projectors, screens, paddling pools and admission tickets were to be funded. Just as he had feared, the mood immediately became more sombre. Bluebell interjected that the movement had only just begun; Snow White, for her part, added that they did have a most capable Robin Hood figure as a fundraiser but that unfortunately he had only recently contrived to shoot himself dead by mistake in a bank basement. Therefore, the position was now vacant and waiting to be filled.

Atam smiled, being somewhat dismayed. The wind blowing over Josefstadt swelled the curtains inwards through the open window until their billowing ceased abruptly and the fabric slid back along the reveal in front of the window recess only to surge again like a spinnaker. The only sound was that of the curtain seams striking the plaster of the walls like a broken metronome; no other time reference existed.

Into this silence, Snow White suddenly asked whether they might set up their headquarters in Atam's apartment. Just then, the balmy wind pushed the curtains aside and a redstart flew in through the open window, chirruping excitedly as it did so; it circled the 1970s glass chandelier as the curtains fell back in front of the window. Then, after three or four such orbits and with the curtains once again blown aside by the wind, it flew back out through the window, into the skies above Piaristengasse.

'Well, if that isn't a sign,' Snow White uttered suddenly. 'That redstart has just sealed our alliance.' She held out her hands to both Atam and Bluebell, and Atam took hold of her hand. Her fingers were warm and somewhat clammy. Slowly, Snow White began to dig her long nails painted blue and silver into his skin. She smiled wryly as she did so, parting her lips to reveal her teeth. She then thrust her jaw forward and shook her head while uttering a prolonged 'Yeah!'

Finally, Snow White stood up without letting go of Atam's hand. He accompanied her to the door and then hurried back to the living room window to wave. He was now alone for the first time in many days and in his own apartment at that. He fetched the cleaning kit for his pistol from the desk, sat down in Snow White's armchair and began disassembling the Browning. Since only one shot had been fired from it, it would be sufficient to brush the barrel. He closed his eyes and could still smell Snow White's unusual, rather metallic perfume, which struck him only now against the backdrop of the smell of gunpowder. And it was to the young woman's steely scent that he promptly fell asleep.

XVI

He later awoke to the sound of softly and cautiously placed footsteps, which he realised were coming from the apartment. He then heard a whispered conversation that immediately elicited a giggle. Lastly, he sensed the smell of vegetable soup and was aware of it being carried over to the dining table. He decided to pretend to be asleep and observe the situation from that particular vantage point. Once the soup bowl had been placed in front of him at the table and the footsteps had receded, he opened his eyes and saw a sparsely laid table in the dimly lit room. He also noticed that the oak floor in the entrance hallway was lit by the kitchen ceiling light, lending a shimmer to its honey tones. From the kitchen itself, he perceived a woman's soft voice. For an instant, he thought he had woken up at Mimi's apartment.

He quickly identified the whispering voices coming from the kitchen as those of Snow White and Bluebell. He checked to make sure all the components of his firearm and its ammunition were still there and then walked over to the kitchen. Snow White and Bluebell were having their soup and looked up without greeting – the way friendly housemates might do – and gave Atam a smile. He noticed that something had changed, that something new and strange had made its way into his flat and was offering up a friendly face to him, at least temporarily; still, he had to take the newness of it into account. And evidently, they had pocketed his apartment keys unnoticed by him as they left, or else they had the ability of surreptitiously breaking into people's apartments. As for getting into the building itself without a key, he himself had demonstrated to them that day as to how it was done. Atam became concerned about the sort of people he had now got involved with and where it might all lead. Once again, it all fitted together somehow; it all stacked up, as if grotesque processes always had reasonable procedures in reality. Was Harmstedter this most capable Robin Hood and fundraiser? You had to be kidding!

As Atam slurped his soup in the parlour, he had to admit to himself that none of it could have come about by chance and that there had to be more to it than that, but he was still unable to detect any malice in any of it; moreover, he refused to see it as part of a larger plot, and at that point his telephone started ringing. Fritz asked where on earth had he been, adding that he had been trying to get hold of him all day. He had messages for him from both Mimi and Andrea and needed an answer.

Mimi wanted to know whether he had finally managed to go shopping that day and when dinner would be ready as she and a friend wanted to attend a pop singer's concert at the Stadthalle at 8 pm and needed a decent meal beforehand. She had to have a solid lining in her stomach so she could go for a drink with her friend after the concert without keeling over;

Andrea, for her part, wanted to know when Atam was finally going to go to her apartment and pack her some things. Fritz was in the process of picking the key up from Uncle László and he would most likely be at Piaristengasse in half an hour's time. He hadn't eaten anything all day either as Mimi had refused him entry first thing in the morning and their regular haunt, the Kaffeehaus Winter, was closed that morning.

Atam promised Fritz some vegetable soup courtesy Snow White, to which Fritz replied: 'Good on you, Atam!' and added 'Respect!' at which point Atam hung up. He wasn't sure if Snow White and Bluebell had left any bread rolls or anything else there was to eat at home, so Atam nipped out to get some groceries from an organic food store on Strozzigasse.

Back home again, he entered his apartment without further ado, opening the door handle with his elbow, having decided in the stairway to go on entering his own flat without ringing the bell, at least during the day. He unpacked his shopping in the kitchen and informed Snow White that someone else would be coming for dinner. Snow White was not amused, pointing out that the soup had been cooked specifically for Atam and not for guests unknown and that, in any case, her sister had already flushed the rest of it down the toilet. With that, she stood up and came very close to Atam, so much so that he involuntarily took a step back and continued to unpack the groceries.

She inspected the apples, picked out a mouldy one, and, with furrowed brow, tossed it into the bin under the sink. She had casually pulled out the bin with her big toe, easing the bottom of the cupboard door. Then, just as casually, she made the bin disappear back under the sink using the ball of her foot, looking to all intents and purposes as if she had actually grown up in that very kitchen. Only then did Atam notice that Snow White was walking barefoot around the apartment. She wore nude-coloured sockettes; one had slipped down completely while the hem of her trouser leg had ridden up, revealing a small band of bare skin at her ankle.

Snow White pulled the farmer's loaf of wholemeal rye out of the paper bag and tossed it angrily onto the countertop. 'That's got gluten in it,' she explained. 'I'm gluten-intolerant. I can't eat that,' she continued menacingly to Atam, who looked at her in surprise. He sought to assuage Snow White by apologising, saying that he was very sorry he hadn't checked with them in advance. But had he at least been right to buy the butter, he inquired of Snow White. 'No, the butter's not right either,' replied Snow White. 'Butter made from unpasteurised milk, straight from the cow, might contain listeria. You've no way of knowing how clean the cows are that the milk comes from,' she told Atam. 'But the cows graze up on mountain pastures,' Atam explained to her. 'And the dairy farmer made the butter up there too and then drove it refrigerated to the shop.' 'No,' Snow White insisted, 'the milk has to be pasteurised beforehand; before you make butter out of it.'

Her expression darkened even more. She went on to explain that gluten affected her period, giving her much shorter yet far more painful periods and that as a result, she feared she might get cancer from the severe and frequent hormonal changes. Atam appeared stunned; he took Snow White's fingers in his hands and kissed them and whispered, 'Please forgive me.' He then took the loaf and tossed it into the rubbish bin under the sink.

Atam asked Snow White to let Fritz in, should he ring the bell before he himself had returned. Then, taking two steps at a time, he hurried back down to Piaristengasse and ran to Strozzigasse to buy gluten free bread and a pack of organic vegetable soup.

When he returned, he found Fritz sitting alone in Snow White's armchair in the living room, staring at the screen of his phone. Atam went straight into the kitchen and handed his new purchases over to Snow White. She took the items matter-of-factly and stowed them away wherever she saw fit without even asking him if those were the right places. Atam noted that he himself was just as indifferent about the whole thing.

He put a saucepan of cold water on the cooker to boil and, to help pass the time, fetched a bottle of sparkling wine from the fridge and carried it into the living room to Fritz, along with several glasses. 'No, no,' he pretended to object. 'We shouldn't, not before sundown.' He grabbed the bottle nonetheless, popped the cork and filled all the champagne glasses that Atam had set out on the tray.

'Thank you; I'll just help myself,' said Fritz, but a moment later he realised something: 'Hang on! There's lipstick on this one! Is that from your new girl? Congratulations!' Atam motioned for Fritz to be quiet. 'I've no idea how that lipstick got on the glass,' he said before going on to correct him. 'She's not my new girl *yet*, for goodness' sake. Plus, she thinks I'm her president, and she wants to be my boss.' 'Mimi also wants to be your boss,' Fritz retorted, adding, 'And, by the way, she's still waiting for your answer.' He gave him a cheeky grin and took a big gulp from the champagne glass.

Atam carried the tray back into the kitchen and served Snow White and Bluebell. Snow White was busy stirring the organic soup powder into the boiling water, her brow furrowed once again. 'Put mine on the table, please, but let me have a sip first,' she ordered, and he let her drink. She emptied the entire glass. 'Not the empty glass!' she chided him, laughing. So, he put the empty glass back on the tray and picked up a full one. But before he could put it down on the table, she said, 'More!' and he served her once again. Finally, she pouted her lips trustingly and said, 'Dab, please.'

Back in the living room, Fritz, still sitting in Snow White's armchair, was refilling Atam's champagne glasses duly emptied by Snow White. He asked what he ought to tell Mimi. After all, he said, it was high time as Mimi would soon be leaving the shop, and then it would be too late for him to cook Mimi something decent. 'You just have your soup,' replied Atam. 'Without bread?' said Fritz. Atam went into the kitchen and cut a slice of the gluten-free farmhouse bread. As he was doing so, Snow White stepped right up to him, almost assaulting him with her half-empty champagne glass, which she pressed to his lips while forcefully preventing him from moving his head away, holding the back of his head with her hand. Atam obediently sipped for as long as she held the glass up to his lips. She did so with meticulous care, at an angle just right for him to drink with ease, so much so that he found himself closing his eyes as she did so. 'There's a good boy,' Snow White praised him.

Fritz pounced on his soup so greedily that he burnt his tongue. He quickly downed some more cold sparkling wine. As he was crumbling the bread between his thumb and forefinger and shaping it into little balls of dough which he threw into the soup, he suddenly had an idea: 'What if we get them all together?' Atam didn't quite follow. 'You know, all your women around one table. Then they can work out which one you should belong to. Or they can divide you up and negotiate rotas for you.'

Atam raised his hands up in the air defensively. 'You've no idea all the commitments I have!' After taking another swig of sparkling wine, Fritz continued unperturbed, 'Listen, that way, everything would be so much clearer, and the women would also be able to plan their lives a lot better. Mimi, for example, has been left hanging right now. What do you want me to write to her? Has your new one even allowed you to go out today?'

XVII

That evening, Snow White relieved Atam of his duties and gave him an hour off to spend time with his visitor. He was even granted permission to accompany him outside the apartment so that she and Bluebell could design the new poster in peace and quiet, provided that Atam was back in time for the meeting. He promised to be home on time and then went to fetch Fritz from the living room. 'I've got two hours, so come on,' he told Fritz.

Once out on Piaristengasse, Atam and Fritz headed northwards at a vigorous pace. 'You really must go to Andrea's apartment now and pack her things so I can take them to the Waldviertel for her. And then you need to go shopping for Mimi and cook her something decent,' said Fritz, summing up the situation in a nutshell. Atam waved his arms about as if that might somehow help to combine the two tasks, adding that he would love to do just that, but had no idea how he was supposed to fit it all into two hours. He pondered whether it would be wiser to drop by Andrea's apartment on the way or whether he should do the shopping and the cooking first and then go and pack Andrea's suitcase. Fritz pointed out that there was a distinct possibility that Mimi might lock Atam inside her apartment again so that he would be at her disposal when she came home from her night out on the town and that therefore it made more sense to pack Andrea's suitcase first.

Atam even considered leaving Mimi out altogether and dedicating himself entirely to Snow White for a while. However, he was not the sort of man who simply dropped a woman before at least establishing some form of mutual agreement with her. By then, they had walked so far as they hurried down Kochgasse towards Alserstrasse that they passed the herb drugstore. Atam raised his arm to indicate the entrance to the shop, but Fritz merely shook his head, adding, 'Forget it, Mimi needs meat!'

By the time Atam was standing outside Andrea's apartment door, he immediately sensed that once again he would be unable to gain access to the premises. And sure enough, even though the key could be inserted smoothly, the cylinder jammed after a quarter-turn and the key remained completely stuck. He let go of the key and, with circumstances being what they were, felt temporarily relieved of Andrea's assignment.

He then wondered where the best place might be to wait for Fritz and the groceries. If he waited where he was, he would lose valuable cooking time; conversely, if he were to leave the premises, he might miss Fritz. So, he decided to at least go back down to the ground floor and walk through the courtyard to the front entrance and wait there. That way, he would gain at least seven minutes. Along the way, he remembered that Fritz had first wanted to take the shopping to Mimi's apartment; and there was really only one sensible way to get from Mimi's apartment to Andrea's, and that was via Brünnlbadgasse. And therefore, in a bid to gain even more time, he decided to walk in the general direction of Mimi's apartment in the hope of encountering Fritz along the way and paid utmost attention to all the pedestrians coming towards him.

He exited the corridor of Andrea's building and soon turned north again on Alserstrasse into Brünnlbadgasse. Very few pedestrians walked past him. But among them was Kosteletzky, of all people, and he wondered whether Gretchen had already dismissed Kosteletzky or whether he, just like Atam, had merely been given time off to complete some errand. They waved to each other across the street and continued on their way. He turned into Gilgegasse, already worrying about running into Mimi, but there was no one to be seen on the street, not even Fritz for that matter.

At the entrance to Mimi's building, Atam pressed all the buzzers and several parties answered one after the other, unlocking the main door for him on a number of occasions, which he could tell from the concert of electric buzzing accompanied by the syncopated snapping of the door lock. He entered the building, flew up the two flights of stairs to Mimi's floor and turned into her corridor. His heart was pounding like that of a child surreptitiously pressed up against a door behind which the Christmas tree stands decorated. Atam listened for the sound of Mimi's footsteps, breathing in the air through the gap in the door. His palpitations persisted, and he had to admit to himself that the mere possibility of encountering Mimi without having yet cooked for her was a worry; still, there was no denying that he also felt a vague yet definite excitement.

Even though he was meant to be back at Snow White's apartment in half an hour, he gave himself an extra hour off, if only to avoid overly spoiling her. Hopefully Kosteletzky had not been on his way home already, otherwise there was a possibility that Gretchen would also want something from him today; he had not the slightest idea how he would begin to accommodate her too in his busy schedule. Anything was possible and right now, everything was up in the air and seemed to depend on Fritz, who, despite his friendly and open demeanour, did not appear to be the most reliable person on the planet.

Another five minutes having elapsed, Atam decided to take control of the situation once again and set off back to Andrea's apartment. As he made his way downhill, he tried to reach Fritz on his phone, but once again, Fritz failed to pick up. Atam quickened his pace. His time buffer had dwindled to eighty minutes and he began to calculate how long he would need to take his leave of Mimi after fulfilling all her unpredictable wishes without upsetting her. Already, it seemed like a hopeless undertaking.

Atam arrived back at Andrea's apartment door without having encountered Fritz on the way there and promptly blamed himself for the same. He went back down to the front entrance on Alserstrasse, resolved this time to actually wait there whatever the circumstances. He was determined not to repeat the same mistake by leaving in a bid to meet him along the way.

By the time his short leave had shrunk to merely sixty-three minutes, he decided to head for the coffeehouse despite his memories of the irritated waitress. Without going to the Gents first, even though he felt a most pressing need to do so, he ordered three meals. He chose vegetable soup, some roast meatloaf with puréed potatoes, and a dessert of flummery with pear halves to go, plus two bottles of *Grüner Veltliner* and a green leaf salad, rinsed but without any dressing. His plan was to dress the salad himself back at Mimi's apartment. While he waited, he ordered a small glass of Nussdorf Gemischter Satz, something he instantly regretted after a couple of sips as a headache began to set in.

There were forty minutes left by the time he stepped back out onto Alserstrasse, clutching the borrowed containers expertly stowed into carrier bags by the waitress. He strode defiantly westwards to Brünnlbadgasse, at which point Fritz finally hove into view. Mimi was not yet home, so Atam transferred his ready-cooked dishes into saucepans, rinsed out the Reindl containers and put them back into the sturdy carrier bags ready to be returned to the coffeehouse, a task Fritz obligingly undertook on Atam's behalf soon thereafter.

XVIII

Atam had a quick look around the apartment. He wondered where all the mess could have come from in just a single day, given that he had left Mimi's flat in perfect order that very morning. He had, after all, cleaned the place thoroughly for days beforehand and done all her laundry. As he busied himself carrying the dirty coffee cups and wine and liqueur glasses into the kitchen, he heard the sound of high heels out in the hallway.

A key was inserted into the lock and the apartment door opened. He saw Mimi smiling beguilingly as she shamefacedly hitched the hem of her short dress even higher. Standing on tiptoe, she walked towards him in something of a *pas de bourrée suivi*. As she did so, she mustered her legs in the large hallway mirror and the play of their muscles and sinews. Her calves stood out rather unattractively, with sharply defined angularity. She covered the rest of the distance across the kitchen floor with a neat *double jeté brisé*, coming to a rather shaky stop directly in front of Atam. This whimsical side of Mimi was something completely new to him. He took hold of her hands as she held each one up to him alternately and kissed each in turn.

Then she disappeared into the bathroom. 'Atam darling,' her voice said sweetly from the bathroom, 'how about an aperitif?' 'On its way,' he replied from the kitchen. As he opened the bathroom door to hand her a glass of sparkling wine, Mimi said, 'Oh, you're so sweet and thoughtful – at the moment, that is. But you never got in touch with me once during the day, did you? With your Mimi, your mistress? You really need to be prodded a little and shown the way, don't you, Atam?'

He removed her clothes from the chair inside the steam-filled bathroom and sorted her skin-toned stockings and white knickers onto the pile of silk laundry as he reached vaguely for her champagne glass with his other hand to refill it. As he did so, he touched her hand, whereupon she immediately grabbed hold of him and pulled him towards her, thrusting her head towards him out from the steamy mist, looking at him lustfully, then pulled his head down to her lips by grabbing his hair, only to push him away again and give his face a little slap. She opined that she fully understood that while Atam might be yearning for his darling Mimi, she had no time for such things right now. And anyway, he had better go and fetch her kimono from the bedroom right away.

When he returned with the desired garment, Mimi was already sitting in her place on the three-seater sofa in the living room, wrapped in a bath towel. 'Atam, you really must remove your shoes when you're walking around here. Don't let me catch you doing that again, understood?' Atam kicked off his shoes by stepping on his heels with the ball of each foot and left the shoes lying on the carpet. Mimi groaned loudly with annoyance. Undeterred, he returned to the kitchen to fetch food. She barely ate any of her vegetable soup, preferring to sip away at her sparkling wine instead.

After the soup, she leaned back, drew her legs up onto the sofa so her heels disappeared under the hem of her kimono, with just her red painted toenails peeking out. Even though a haze of appetising flavours was rising up from the plate with the meatloaf, she leaned right back on the sofa, turned onto her side, closed her eyes and promptly began to snore softly. Atam's stomach stirred once again so he pulled her plate towards him and ate all its contents, sipping from her champagne glass all the while until it was completely empty.

It was in the midst of this idyll that his phone began to ring. He tried to pick up quickly so as to not disturb Mimi, but she did wake up nonetheless and extended her hand, asking for the phone. Atam, somewhat perplexed, did not hand it over immediately so she waved her fingers tantalisingly with the merest hint of a smile on her lips until Atam handed Mimi his phone, at which point her smile instantly vanished. 'Who is this and why are you interrupting?' Mimi asked sternly. 'Oh, it's you, Fritz! How dare you call at this time?' She hung up and asked Atam if he had enjoyed his meal because she was still hungry.

As Atam hurried into the kitchen to get another portion of meatloaf, his phone rang a second time and once again, Mimi answered rather sharply. It was Snow White calling from Fritz's phone, demanding to speak to Atam. She made it clear that she had no intention whatsoever of making herself known to whoever had just answered his phone on his behalf and that it was no business of theirs why she wanted to speak to Atam; after all, Atam belonged to her, i.e., Snow White, since he was her president, and they were all far too busy right now trying to save the world.

This appeared to assuage Mimi: 'Well, if you're saving the world, don't let me interrupt you. Call back in an hour, why don't you?' She hung up and tossed the phone onto the coffee table just as Atam came in with her plate of freshly prepared, yet lukewarm, meatloaf and served it to her. 'You know,' Mimi began, 'When I say I need a proper meal because I'm going to a concert and want to have a drink afterwards, it would be nice of you not to eat everything off my plate and then serve me the cold leftovers with that innocent and wide-eyed look of yours.' Mimi held up her empty glass, adding, 'Just pour me some wine, will you?'

Atam braced himself for what might well lie in store whenever Mimi, tired and tense from her day, emptied two glasses of sparkling wine and half a glass of wine before eating, being apparently in a foul mood. And yet, he could not help informing Mimi, in all honesty, that he was not looking for praise for his cooking skills, especially since he had not even cooked but had merely fetched the pre-prepared food from the coffeehouse and had simply re-heated everything so it could be served hot. He added that Mimi had then promptly fallen asleep, something he could do little about other than eating her lukewarm meal himself so the loud rumbling of his stomach would not wake her. Mimi let Atam finish his little tirade, staring intently at his face, further unsettling him. And indeed, once he had finished his explanations, he found himself biting his lower lip rather sheepishly. Sure enough, Mimi took a deep breath and pursed her lips, yet uttered only, 'Atam, you are an imbecile.'

She then demanded dessert and, in yet another dig at him, asked rhetorically whether she could expect the dessert to be lukewarm too. Fortunately, Atam was able to douse the flummery with some high-octane fruit brandy and serve it flambéed. No, Mimi did not want coffee served with it but a liqueur and some more sparkling wine; after all, she had to get her body fine-tuned for her bar visit later that evening.

Chuckling to herself, she stabbed at the burning flummery and scooped out a spoonful for Atam to taste. 'Here, try it for me!' she ordered and, dutifully, he opened his mouth wide to receive the morsel that was still aglow. He blew hard on it to cool it as he did so, spraying some of the burning brandy in Mimi's general direction. Mimi shrieked, tossed the half-eaten burning spoonful aside and slapped Atam so hard that the piece of flummery he had bitten off flew out of his mouth, albeit it was by now quenched.

'Are you trying to flambé me too?' asked Mimi in a rage. Atam grabbed the full champagne glass and emptied it over Mimi. She stood up without a word, slapped Atam again – this time with the back of her hand – and ordered him to make sure he had all the mess cleared up by the time she came back. She went on to complain about the fact that she would now have to trawl the bars hungry and on an empty stomach in order to still her anger and that he only had himself to blame if she came home very late and in a state such that she would be unable to offer him later on any of the things that a woman otherwise might.

Atam proceeded to clear away what remained of the failed meal and made a start on tidying up the kitchen. Then he heard Mimi yelling from the bathroom, asking him where her clothes were and whether even that was now too much to ask of him, namely organising something nice for her to wear. And so, Atam left the dishes unwashed, hurried over to Mimi's walk-in closet with all her clothes and began to put together an outfit for her big night out, laying everything out for her on the bed.

She hurried into the room wearing her kimono and, while surveying the garments, undressed in front of Atam, handing him her bathrobe to put away. She had already done her hair in the bathroom and attended to her make-up too. His choice of garments seemed to meet with her approval since she wordlessly put on what Atam had laid out for her. Before she slipped into her blouse, he adjusted one of her bra straps that had become twisted. She watched him closely as he did so. 'You really are very sweet,' she said. 'I certainly won't be giving you back. Wait up for me, won't you? I'll try and hurry.' He helped her into her blouse and turned down the collar. While Mimi sat teasing out her hair with her fingers and checking her make-up in a dusty hand mirror, Atam helped her into her knee-highs. Taking her feet in his hands, he warmed them first and massaged the toes one by one before slipping on the socks. As he slid one elasticated hem up her calf, he applied a little too much force and caught her leg, causing her knee to bump up against her elbow as she was re-applying her mascara. 'Can't you be more careful?' Mimi snapped. 'You'll be giving me a black eye next!'

She checked her face one final time in the dusty hand mirror that he must have overlooked and forgotten to clean. She grunted in self-appreciation, jumped up, gazed languidly up into his eyes by way of farewell, stood on tiptoe to close the

the distance between their eyes and then ran out of the door without even a kiss, locking him in as she did so, something he only noticed after she had called out from the stairwell to book her a taxi and he had tried to open the door to shout 'Jawohl!' after her. He then heard the ever-diminishing staccato sound of her heels as she made her way down the stairs.

XIX

'Four minutes,' the soothing and trustworthy female voice informed Atam by way of a reply. But even before he could thank her, his telephone rang and as he held it away from his ear to see who was calling, the operator hung up, automatically connecting Andrea to the freed-up line.

She whispered beautiful words into the microphone of her telephone and Atam endeavoured to respond with similarly beautiful words in order to not spoil the scene she had evidently staged for herself. Then, out of nowhere, Andrea enquired as to his precise whereabouts in her apartment, and while he pondered the potential consequences of an all too frank answer to her question, a woman's footsteps could be heard approaching along the corridor, prompting Andrea to enquire whether he had brought the same woman home again or whether it was someone new?

Atam answered sincerely that he was indeed alone and that a woman had simply passed by outside in the corridor. He then went on to state in his usual fearless and honest way that he was not actually at home in Andrea's apartment. He had had to bring Mimi a pre-cooked meal as she wanted to go to a pop concert after work and did not have time to cook for herself. He could tell Andrea was listening to him intently. She then exhaled deeply, wetted her lips and took her next breath before hanging up. He immediately dialled her number and her phone rang, but Andrea did not pick up, and the connection was finally disconnected by the telephone exchange after it had been left to ring for a long time. Atam redialled and then dialled once more, and this time he was lucky: Andrea picked up and apologised for not answering before. She went on to add that she had certainly heard it ringing but could not pick up as she was too upset and needed to relax with a yoga exercise. What's more, the Brigadier had been standing next to her, eager to intervene to calm her down as he had noticed that she had been traumatised by the phone call.

Atam replied that Andrea had nothing to apologise for, at which point she immediately chipped in to say that he had not done anything either, nothing at all in fact, to alter yesterday's situation and that he must therefore obviously be very comfortable with it and that was something she simply had to come to terms with; further, he ought to know that she was so terribly hurt by it all that she was unable to talk about it any further and that Atam should forgive her for hanging up right now as something inside her had been shattered and she now had to force herself to return to her duties without letting anything show. And with that, Andrea hung up.

Atam now found himself cornered, so he decided simply to satisfy Andrea's needs from Mimi's wardrobe selection. After all, both women had a similar figure. He picked out everything that was on Andrea's list, persuading himself that certain variations would be permissible and that, in any case, there were no flashy garments among them, no 14th century heirlooms as there might have been with his own grandmother; rather, it was all conventional prêt-à-porter. He laid everything out carefully on the coffee table in the living room. Next, he went in search of suitcases. Under Mimi's bed, he found two white on-board cases made of lightweight plastic. They had been left there with their lids open and were all dusty inside, with a light sprinkling of all kinds of crumbs. He turned the suitcases over, tapped them out onto the carpet before finally wiping them clean with a damp cloth.

He then called Fritz, but as usual, Fritz was not answering his phone. So, he wrote him a text message saying that he had fulfilled Andrea's instructions and asked him to come to Mimi's to collect the suitcases as Mimi had once again locked him inside the apartment, as was now the standard procedure. A short while later his phone beeped with a message from Fritz. It said that, unfortunately, the cavalry would not be arriving promptly today for, once again, Snow White was refusing to let Fritz leave the apartment until Atam had returned home.

He telephoned the Winter coffeehouse. Initially, the waitress was not terribly enthusiastic about his plans, but once Atam had explained to her that an acquaintance of his in the Waldviertel was urgently in need of a change of clothes and that he, however, had been locked inside someone else's apartment just around the corner by another acquaintance while the driver assigned to fetch the clothes was himself being held prisoner in his own apartment by a third acquaintance, her golden Viennese heart shone through and she agreed to walk to Mimi's courtyard so Atam could throw his keys down to her through the bedroom window and she could take them by taxi to Piaristengasse and toss them up to Fritz; after all, it was not the sort of thing that taxi drivers could either be required or trusted to do.

And indeed, after Atam had washed Mimi's jumper in a fast wash for woollens and was in the process of unloading the machine, Fritz was already ringing the doorbell, barely half an hour later. Not even the small suitcase could fit through the grille in the kitchen window facing out onto the corridor. Fritz was dead against Atam simply throwing the suitcases down into the courtyard, and so, he suggested that Atam lower the suitcases using sheets knotted together. There was a small mishap with the larger suitcase due to its heavy weight. A knot got caught on the outer window sill and, as Atam tried to push it beyond the outer lip of the sheet metal ledge, it broke loose and the suitcase plunged down the last few metres onto Fritz, along with the sheets now ripped apart as they twirled their way to the ground like a gyrating Chinese dragon.

XX

It was already very late – close to midnight in fact – when he was woken by the percussive sound of high heels in the corridor. They sounded almost elegant, as if floating, even though Mimi's strides were never as ample and forthright as his mother's had been in the past whenever she returned home from the opera, her head still spinning from a wonderful evening spent in pleasant company and several glasses of champagne at the interval. Through his window, which he kept open in all weathers, he would listen out intently into the street all evening until, with a loudly beating heart, he finally perceived her long awaited return by the rhythmic tilting of her high heels. They elicited in him a sweet anticipation of the embrace that would soon be his. Still, he had to endure the torture of the overly long wait as she walked up the five storeys and discarded her hat and gloves in the hallway, only then finally entering his room and hugging him in a fragrant cloud of Elizabeth Arden's *Blue Grass*. Mimi, for her part, smelled rather of pub kitchens and, by way of greeting, slapped him.

He recalled how his mother had warned him about women. 'Atam,' she had said when he was still in primary school and his interest in girls was becoming obvious, (Indeed, she had once been summoned by the headmaster because he had disappeared from class to press himself up against the black iron grille in front of the Blessed Virgin Mary in the aisle outside the chapel with a girl from a higher year.) 'Beware of women, and do not trust them.'

With his cheek still ringing with the slap, he helped Mimi out of her blazer and hung it in front of the window to air. Visibly touched by his thoughtful gesture, she managed a smile that oscillated between tiredness and excitement. She gently raised the hand that had just slapped him and patted his reddened cheek with the back of her hand, which was still cooled by the chill of the night. The little bells dangling from her bracelet resounded like something out of the *Arabian Nights*. Then she turned her hand around and drove her nails into Atam's other cheek, shaking his face and crying out in rapture, 'My dear little Atam, you're ever so sweet. What would I do without you?' With that, she retracted her hand once more, albeit not as amply as previously and softly slapped Atam's face with the palm of her hand, the rustic ring on her ring finger striking him painfully nonetheless.

Again, she dragged him by the hand into the living room and flopped down onto the sofa, manoeuvring him onto his knees in front of her. Once Atam had slipped off her shoes, she put her legs up on the coffee table with a huge sigh of relief next to a jumper that had not found room inside the suitcase. She stared at Atam's face in mock disbelief, her chin demandingly hinting towards the general direction of her feet. Atam instantly understood and took each of her toes in turn, squeezing and stroking each one upwards towards its joint. Next, he tugged on each of the toes once again, as if about to pull each one off, before bending them again along their joints. Mimi groaned with pleasure and pointed encouragingly at her feet one more time, staring fixedly at Atam as she did so. He leaned forward, his eyes trained firmly on her and with her nod of encouragement leaving him in no doubt, he pulled her lace socks off her feet and began sucking each of her toes in turn.

Mimi threw back her head and smiled contentedly until her stomach began to rumble. 'That,' Mimi said, 'is entirely your fault. I'm hungry, and I'm really feeling the alcohol in my stomach because you didn't feed me properly. What kind of man are you that you cannot feed a woman?' Atam wanted to get up and make her something to eat, but Mimi shook her head vigorously, and so, Atam remained kneeling before her toes and continued to massage them until she fell asleep, which he only noticed once she began to snore. 'How far we've come,' Atam thought. Even though he knew what had happened the last time, he pulled her legs up onto the sofa and placed a cushion under her back before creeping quietly out into the hallway to rummage through Mimi's handbag in search of the apartment key.

As he descended the stairs, he felt a sadness at leaving Mimi, but the further he got from her building, the more that feeling gave way to an increasing anticipation of seeing Snow White. At Jodok-Fink-Platz, the Maria Treu coffeehouse opposite the basilica, was still open and so, Atam entered, exuberant from the smooth success of his escape, and drank a full glass of Grüner Veltliner white wine, standing at the counter while the waiter busied himself counting the day's takings. Thus fortified, he strode forcefully towards his own apartment building and rang the intercom three times in quick succession as he had learnt to do from Andrea when she had buzzed Uncle László at Flötzersteig.

Snow White answered in a flat toneless voice, asking rather rudely who it was, and when Atam answered, 'Your ruler,' she wordlessly pressed the door release. The apartment door was ajar, but there was no one waiting to greet him. His primary objective now was to release Fritz so he could take Mimi's clothes to Andrea, and so, he walked into the living room, but Fritz was nowhere to be seen. Snow White and Bluebell were sitting at the table, bent over a multitude of sheets of paper. It was not until he had almost reached the table that Snow White actually stood up and hesitantly took three half-steps towards him.

Stopping some distance away from him, she scrutinised him closely. Without holding out her hand, she took a final half-step closer. She sniffed his breath, walked around him and asked, 'Have you been drinking?' Atam nodded and replied, 'A large Grüner Veltliner at the counter at Maria Treu.' At that, Snow White wrinkled her nose contemptuously, shook her head and gave Atam a resounding slap in the face on the very same cheek that had only recently been stinging from Mimi's slap.

Not entirely surprised, Atam stroked his cheek, barely able to suppress a grin. He asked Snow White as the apparent new keeper of his apartment where Fritz might be. She pointed towards the door of Atam's bedroom and explained that she had kept Fritz locked up in there while she awaited Atam's return, safe and sound, even if 'safe and sound' was perhaps not the *mot juste* for someone in such a drunken state; so, Fritz would have to remain locked in until Atam had sobered up.

With some amusement, Atam followed Snow-White into the bedroom. No sooner had he entered the room than Snow White slammed the bedroom door shut behind him and locked him in too.

XXI

After much shaking of hands, Fritz pointed his chin at the two on-board suitcases on the bed. He furrowed his brow and raised his shoulders questioningly. 'I had no choice but to come back and wait for you here. I felt it was my duty and my obligation.' Atam sat down on the edge of his king-sized bed, next to the suitcases, and distractedly ran his hand over their rounded surface. He then went over to the window and looked down into the courtyard. 'Fritz,' he began, 'You're going to have to rope yourself down using the bed sheets.'

Fritz shook his head in denial. Still, Atam placed the suitcases in front of the window, pulled the bedspread off the bed and used a reef knot to tie the quilt cover to the bedspread. He then quickly knotted the cover of the second quilt to the large bedsheet. He tied the makeshift rope to the radiator under the window and tested its tensile strength by leaning back into the room with all his weight while holding on to the rope. And while the radiator moved a few millimetres and creaked in its anchoring, it held fast. He tossed the makeshift rope of bed sheets out of the window. 'You'll just have to jump the last few metres.'

Fritz argued that he would rather try and negotiate with Snow White. However, he had little to offer by way of objection to Atam's interjection that Snow White had just slapped him hard and still appeared very disgruntled. And when Atam also pointed out that Andrea would be furious if Fritz did not bring her the clothes that very day, he did finally swing himself over the windowsill. With his legs braced at a 90° angle against the façade, he deftly rappelled down the façade half a metre at a time until the rope ran out and then dropped to the ground.

Atam pulled the rope back in and after briefly listening at the bedroom door to make sure all was still quiet in the living room, he untied the knot from the radiator. Once he had placed the small suitcase on the windowsill ready to lower it down by the sheets, he suddenly realised he had to rope both suitcases down at the same time; otherwise, how was he supposed to retrieve the rope after dropping off the first suitcase, complete with rope? And so, he immediately fed the end of the rope through the handle of the second suitcase, too, and then lifted them both out together and lowered them as far as the rope would go. 'Watch out!' he half-shouted. He then let go and quickly shut the window so Snow White would not be alerted by the sound of the impact and become suspicious.

He walked over to the door and listened in again, but all was still perfectly quiet in his apartment. Nonetheless, he switched off the light as a precaution and crept over to his bed in the dark, collapsing with relief on top of it. Then, just as he was about to drift off to sleep, he rose once more, stripped to his underwear and, after folding his clothes neatly over a chair, slipped under the quilt. In the semi-darkness, half sitting up and leaning against the headboard, he craned his neck slightly so he could stare out through the closed window into the courtyard illuminated by the corridor light. Once the light had gone out, he lay back and relaxed fully, staring up at the bedroom ceiling. But right there, beside the ceiling light, he spotted a dark and slightly raised stain and resolved to clean it once it was daylight again. And it was with this minor plan in mind that he fell fast asleep, exhausted from the day's events.

He could not have been asleep for more than an hour and a half when his phone began to vibrate. Fighting his immense fatigue, Atam quickly crawled out of bed to his clothes on the chair and hastily searched through all his pockets. He found his device in the last pocket, on the wrong side, next to the pistol magazine, and answered the call by touching the illuminated button.

Such were the pleasant susurrations and sounds of delight with which Andrea was now immersing him over the phone that he found himself smiling in the darkness. Several times during the short pauses that Andrea needed to catch her breath, he tried unsuccessfully to respond in equally dulcet tones. He feared she might lurch to the other extreme at any moment. And indeed, he was not disappointed in this regard. By the time Andrea had enquired a second time, rather impatiently, whether he felt the task assigned to him had been that difficult and she had commented that he did seem capable after all of doing things right when he put his mind to it, he knew he was in trouble.

Before Atam could object that it was not his fault if Andrea had given him the wrong key (he was reluctant to mention the fact that Uncle László's key hadn't worked either as that would have meant having to explain to Andrea that she was now wearing Mimi's clothes), Andrea interpreted his gentle silence as an admission, adding: 'So you see, my Atamo, it's all really quite simple, and all's well that ends well.' Never before had Andrea called him Atamo. However, she then got to the point, saying that she had begun to wonder, understandably, whether, in light of his tardiness of some two days, a relationship with a man not even willing to fetch her own clothes from her own apartment was in fact good for her.

Whispering softly, Atam replied that he would make a terrible husband and that Andrea would do well to give him a wide berth and that he would fully understand were she to do so for he was not worthy of her. His admission of unsuitability triggered such a sense of satisfaction in Andrea that she instantly gained the upper hand, mellowing to a state of gentle disposition in which she held out the prospect of reprieve. Atam swallowed loudly. Whereupon she asked him why he had become so quiet. Had he nothing more to say? After all, she had just given him one more—utterly undeserved—opportunity to redeem himself. Atam was about to answer in a tone of moderation when Andrea interjected that she failed to understand how could it be that, given the importance of what she was saying about their relationship, he himself had nothing to add on the matter. How could it be that someone who had not only not been able to bring her any clothes from her own apartment – there had never been any talk of buying her new clothes, so he would never have had to go to any personal expense and in any case, she could always provide for herself; in fact, hadn't she immediately managed to find herself a new job? Also, he – had then gone to another woman, a total stranger, and had cooked for her and was now simply absorbing all her justified doubts without comment? That really was one step too far. And why was he constantly trying to interrupt her, she wondered, as he sought to take advantage of her loudly drawing breath by uttering her name just at the moment she inhaled?

'Well?' she asked, and Atam proceeded cautiously to point out that Andrea had given him the wrong key, but that was all he needed to say. From tenderness, Andrea instantly tilted into a state of deepest hurt and disappointment. She went on to say that she was someone who always gave herself completely, who had always given so much more in love than she had ever received in return, sacrificing herself entirely for the man's sake. Without a second's hesitation, she would have been willing to throw herself in front of him to shield him with her own body and take any bullet fired at him and die for him. And yet this very man, whose indifference had left her in the freezing cold and forced her to expose herself in front of her new employer, was now also making her out to be a complete fool who only had herself to blame for her feelings of hurt after she had dropped everything for him in order to flee the police with him.

And with that, Andrea fell silent, a silence so loud that Atam became spooked by it. In order not to irritate her any further, he pleaded guilty once again, and it was at that moment that Snow White opened the bedroom door, switched on the light and found Atam in his underpants, shading his blinded eyes with one hand while holding the mobile phone to his ear with the other. With a cold fury filled with reproach, she asked who he was talking to, given that she had locked him in to sober up. She then looked around the room and asked where Fritz was.

Before he could answer, she suddenly yelled at him not to come a step closer. Andrea, for her part, yelled into the phone, demanding to know about the woman Atam was now cheating on her in Mimi's apartment and whether he had no decency whatsoever. She was grateful to the heavens that her eyes had been opened as soon as they had and that she had now lost all faith in men.

Atam had to placate Snow White as she seemed capable of just about anything and so, he informed her firmly and resolutely that Fritz had abseiled out the window with the knotted bed sheets as he was desperate to take some warm clothes to Andrea in the Waldviertel. A silence began to fill Atam's bedroom during which he retrieved a pillow from the bed to cover up his nether regions.

Snow White grabbed the phone from his hand. 'Hello? Who's that?' she demanded. 'The time for hellos has passed,' Andrea replied combatively and loudly, adding in a whispered tone, 'It's me, Andrea.' Snow White retorted, 'Right now, we have more important things to deal with than a "domestic". We still have to save the world. Is it true that Fritz is with you?' 'No, he's gone already,' Andrea replied loudly and, with a show of anger, hung up.

Snow White told Atam that his girlfriend did not seem very helpful. At that, Atam bristled. On the contrary, he explained, Andrea was not even his girlfriend and yet, for his sake, she would have been prepared to die for him. She had said as much, shortly before Snow White had interrupted their conversation. Such a woman could hardly be called unhelpful.

Unmoved, Snow White retorted that anyone could say that sort of a thing and that many people had offered verbally to die sacrificial deaths but were still alive and well to this day. Atam protested only mildly as he was glad that Snow White now seemed to be willing to talk to him like a normal human being again. Feeling that a minor hysterical fit might tug at her heart strings even further, he threw himself onto the bed, wiggling his legs, and buried his head in his arms, sobbing so bitterly and loudly that the whole of his body was shaking. Snow White stood perfectly still, showing not the slightest hint of sympathy, and so, he slowly let himself drift back out of his little performance.

She waited with her arms folded as he sat back up in bed, wiping the tears of his dramatic antics from his eyes while looking defiantly at Snow White's face. Shaking her head, she turned on her heel and left the room but not without locking the door behind her once again. Atam heard her footsteps receding all the way into the living room from where he perceived Bluebell asking, 'Is everything okay? You alright?'

XXII

Atam crept over to the door to eavesdrop and peep through the keyhole. Only then did he realise that quite evidently, Snow White had changed her clothes and was now wearing a green minidress with orange stripes. He heard her say that Atam, despite his harmless and innocent appearance, must be as cunning as a fox. 'What do you mean "cunning"?' asked Bluebell. 'He's a sly old dog,' Snow White explained. 'Well, he's certainly no spring chicken,' remarked Bluebell.

Retrospectively, Atam realised that Snow White was wearing specially designed orthopaedic shoes with her silk stockings. At the toe, they consisted of two articulated soles pushed apart at the heel by strong copper spirals, creating a springy high heel. With each downward step, the shoe would contract and clack just as it clacked when released with each upward step; it meant that every stride she took with this orthopaedic footwear was accompanied by a double clack and somehow that suited her temperament admirably.

Presently, Snow White had, for all intents and purposes, calmed down and was again sitting next to Bluebell in what had once been his living room. Now only the occasional louder sound could be heard from the otherwise muffled chatter between the two women, dampened by doors and distance, and so, Atam found himself once again entirely alone in the peace and quiet of his bedroom. He thought of Mimi, who presumably was still sleeping with her bare feet on the coffee table as he had forgotten to cover her legs with a blanket. He wondered how much he had improved his situation ever since he had broken free of Mimi's captivity, and it occurred to him that he had at least been able to send Andrea some of Mimi's clothes and enjoy a large glass of wine at the counter at the Maria Treu coffeehouse. Pleased at the thought, he slipped back under the covers and fell asleep.

There is no way of telling whether Snow White simply forgot to keep his phone or whether she later changed her mind; in any case, she had not taken his phone away from him. Which is why, an hour and a half or so later, Atam was again roused from his slumber by his vibrating phone. He crawled out of bed to fetch his phone, which was tucked into his clothes neatly folded on the chair, and answered the call.

Sleepily, he whispered into the microphone, but no one answered. He could also sense a familiar perfume – at least a fragrance he had sensed recently – and an electrifying feeling of unease overcame him deep down. He took a short step towards the window to improve the connection, but still he could hear nothing and so, in the end, he hung up and went back towards the bed. Then, suddenly, the light came on and Snow White shoved him firmly in the chest, propelling him onto the bed. At the same time, Bluebell leapt panther-like onto the bed next to him, catapulting him off the sprung mattress and snatching the phone from his fingers. She immediately turned around and dashed nimbly back to the door and disappeared giggling.

With the mattress still bouncing ever so slightly, Atam realised that Snow White and Bluebell had probably just been pretending to have a cosy chat amongst themselves while, in reality, they had lulled him into a false sense of security; indeed, they must have assumed he would be listening at the door. These thoughts unsettled him. He also had a dark foreboding of what further complications might arise should Andrea, Gretchen or Mimi choose to call him. And he could only hope that Fritz would start to worry once he had not heard from Atam in a while.

Thereafter, he lay in bed tossing and turning and kept waking up from a restless sleep. And each time, he had to reorientate himself as to where he was and when. Then, in a flash, he would grasp the full impact of his situation, only to forget all about it immediately afterwards. At one point he sat bolt upright in his bed in a cold sweat, intending to do something – anything at all – to get Snow White and Bluebell out of his apartment. And that was when he heard a chinking noise at the window. He was reluctant to get up, but the noise persisted intermittently. As he opened the window, a one-euro coin flew into the room in a silent yet perfect parabola and landed on the carpet with a dull thud.

'Fritz?' enquired Atam cautiously down into the courtyard. 'Of course, it's me!' Fritz replied. 'Who else do you think would be throwing money at your window? Marilyn Monroe?' Fritz asked how he was – a little too loudly for Atam's liking. Without waiting for Atam's reply, he went on to say that after dinner, he had tried umpteen times call him, without success, and had therefore become worried about what the two dames had done to him. It had, however, taken him longer to get into the building as the front entrance door was locked and for tactical reasons, he had not wanted to ring the bell. It took him a while to finally realise that you could simply push open the main entrance door by ringing the buzzer of a doctor's surgery.

'Fritz, when it gets light, go and fetch Mimi as back-up and tell her that Snow White is plotting to steal her Atam away from her; she's bound to come and rescue me.' Fritz could not think of a better way out of this predicament either; after all, he himself was unable to drive the women from the apartment, neither by force nor by trickery. Mimi, however, would have no inhibitions in this regard.

It seemed to be a speciality of Snow White's and Bluebell's to prepare food in his kitchen unnoticed and serve it to him without waking him. Indeed, he later woke to the warm and intense aroma of coffee and caught sight of a full breakfast tray laid out on the chair from which his clothes had been removed. He sat up and pulled the tray onto his lap. The coffee tasted bitter, and he instantly became suspicious that Snow White had put some sleeping draught or other into the coffee. He quickly let the coffee flow back out of his mouth into the cup and spat a few times.

As his stomach was rumbling, he decided to at least satiate his hunger. As he sat camped out in his bed, bare-chested (for under the covers he was wearing nothing other than his underpants), unwashed and unshaven for several days now, a feeling of fullness in his lower abdomen as he ate alerted him to the fact that he had not yet had a chance to go to the toilet properly. He put the tray back on the chair and got up to go to the bathroom. On the way there, he nurtured the faint hope that the two siblings had vanished for good and had brought him breakfast in bed by way of reparation; but no, the door was still locked.

He rattled the door handle, knocked on the door and called out into the morning silence that he urgently needed to use the bathroom and that they had had their fun and could stop now. But he got no answer. He pummelled the bedroom door with his fists, so much so that the door leaf began to rattle and vibrate. Apart from his shouting, the pounding of his fists and the shaking of the door, there was silence throughout the apartment and, in fact, the whole building. Once, very briefly, he thought he heard some giggling – Bluebell's perhaps – but it must have been the sound of a car braking hard on Piaristengasse.

His stomach began to rumble in earnest and he felt a slight cramping in his abdomen. He rushed over to the window and climbed onto the window sill, where he knelt down. With one hand grasping the impost above his head, he used the other to free his member from his underwear and direct it outwards. Just as he was relieving himself, he heard noises from the hallway. Then, the bedroom door flew open, and he could hear a rather anxious voice call out his name.

XXIII

'Don't jump!' shouted Fritz as he rushed over to the window, grabbing Atam by the waist and falling back into the room with him. Mimi shrieked and giggled merrily: 'Looks like you really have just come down off the mountains.' She then picked a pillow off the bed and threw it at Atam, who was lying on his back on the floor, fully exposed. He managed to cover up his nether regions. With the pillow held in front of him, he got up and marched off to the bathroom. In the meantime, Mimi and Fritz rummaged through the apartment in search of Atam's clothes and found them neatly folded and intact in the American girls' bedroom.

Atam entered the living room badly shaved and with a bit of toilet paper stuck to the razor cut on his cheek, much to Mimi's displeasure. 'Really?' she rebuked him. 'Can't you do anything right, not even shave? What kind of a man are you? You pee out of the window like some ruffian. What will people think? I hope no one I know saw you!' She poured out some coffee. He thanked her and took his cup, which she held onto for longer than was strictly necessary so his hand would touch her fingers. It was a gesture of tenderness that comforted him for her harsh words, which – knowing Mimi as he now did – were never to be taken at face value. And in any case, a sense of contentment began to set in the instant he had taken his first few sips of hot coffee.

Footsteps could then be heard out in the corridor and just as Mimi was reprimanding her boys yet again, a key was forcefully inserted into the lock and the door was pushed open. Marching through the hallway, the sisters strode into the living room, holding hands. Letting go of Snow White's hand, Bluebell clapped her hands and let out a loud laugh. 'Here he is!' she said before hurrying over to Fritz, hugging him effusively and then pushing him away the very next moment.

Mimi remained seated and finished her coffee in one gulp. Then she got up, stepped forward and held her hand out to Snow White by way of greeting. Snow White reached out and was immediately thrown to the ground. She landed on her stomach on the carpet, with Mimi pinning her down by twisting her outstretched arm behind her. 'Good morning, Miss Secretary. I thought I'd given you permission to talk to my boy on the phone for an hour and no more,' she said. She then stretched her left hand out towards Bluebell and gave her an impish smile. Against her better judgement, Bluebell reached out, but before she could even reply, she too found herself lying on the floor next to Snow White, in the same physical predicament.

Years of attending jiu-jitsu classes in the hope of meeting a more rugged type of man had seemingly paid off. Mimi twisted both arms even tighter to lend emphasis to her little performance. The half-sisters began to wail in pain, but

Mimi commanded them to be silent. Once they had stopped whimpering, she lectured them that Atam and Fritz belonged to her and that if it ever occurred to them to interfere with her boys again, she would break every bone in their bodies. To back up her threat, she twisted their arms even more until there was a loud crack and the sisters yelped. She then let go of their arms, sat down again and signalled to Atam to pour her out some more coffee.

The siblings gingerly got back to their feet, tugged their clothes into place and went and stood silently in the window alcove with reddened faces. Only now did Atam notice that the siblings had changed yet again since the previous night and must have a plentiful supply of clothes at their disposal in the bedroom they were using in his apartment. Mimi got ready to go back to her shop and instructed Atam to call her if there was any trouble. Atam intimated that he would love to call her but that Bluebell had confiscated his phone the previous night.

Once Mimi had pulled the apartment door shut with her foot and her footsteps had echoed away down the corridor, the mood within the apartment changed abruptly and Atam offered the sheepishly subdued siblings some coffee. Snow White ran her hands down her dress to smooth it out and then attended to her hair. Bluebell, now emboldened, poked at her messy bun and asked, 'What about breakfast?'

So there they sat, with the window looking out onto Piaristengasse wide open and the curtains once again billowing in the wind that blew into the room more forcefully than the previous day, given that both the bedroom windows and the doors in between were open. Now that the difficult night seemed to be over, the lighter mood of the previous afternoon returned, spreading to all and sundry, including Fritz this time. Then, suddenly, both bedroom doors slammed shut at once due to the draught, hitting the strike plates with a loud crash.

Bluebell jumped with a start, giggled and was the first to start laughing, with Atam then joining in, followed by Snow White while Fritz smiled good-naturedly even though, like the others, he was not quite sure what he was laughing at. This outburst of unfounded merriment appeared to clear the air completely. In the end, Bluebell leapt up and disappeared into her room. She could be heard rummaging around and singing something to herself. Soon she returned carrying a multitude of paper scrolls under her arms. Everyone helped to clear space on the table and spread out the rolls of paper. The coffee cups were used as paperweights to prevent the sheets from curling up again. Fritz was now the one to laugh heartily as the uppermost poster featured a naked man who looked exactly like Atam, kneeling in a small inflatable paddling pool and holding his hands in the water with his arms outstretched as if trying to scoop the pool empty with his bare fingers.

His genitals, too, appeared to be depicted in the utmost detail, prompting Fritz to ask rather teasingly whether it was possible to draw a member so accurately without actually having seen it in the flesh. Without answering, Snow White rolled up the poster with the naked Atam, revealing a poster with Fritz underneath, albeit with privates undepicted. 'She who laughs last laughs loudest,' said Bluebell, interrupting Fritz's laughter. Then, turning towards him, she added, 'Now strip off.'

The laughter instantly drained from his face. He had not forgotten that the two sisters had locked him in, that they had behaved badly towards him right from the outset, and that it was because of them that he had had to abseil down from the second floor. To play for time and get himself in the mood, he asked for wine, and so, Snow White instructed Atam to go and buy some wine as supplies in the apartment had been depleted. Atam pointed out that Snow White was teetotal.

She brushed the objection aside with an expansive gesture that swept several scrolls of paper right off the table, pointing out that she herself was not at all anti-alcohol and was by no means teetotal and that the anger she had displayed yesterday had been directed solely at Atam for disappointing her by coming home tipsy from another woman for whom he had cooked while bringing her a loaf of highly toxic bread. She added that now was the ideal time for Fritz to demonstrate what stuff he was made of and that if he felt he could fulfil that task more easily if slightly inebriated, then the use of alcohol would certainly be more than apposite.

As Atam readied himself to go out and fetch a couple of bottles from the Maria Treu, Fritz started yelling that Atam must not leave him there alone with the two women. Atam, too, was keen to take Fritz along with him to help carry the bottles, but Snow White saw right through him, remarking that it would no doubt suit them both to be able to disappear and that such a thing was out of the question. So either Fritz stripped off right there and then without the benefit of imbibing some wine first, or Atam could go and fetch the wine on his own.

Atam then asked where his gun was, stating that if only for legal reasons, the half-sisters were obliged to hand it over to him. As they did not answer straight away even though they had understood his question perfectly well, he suddenly had an inkling that his gun might play a bigger role in the whole story. It was then that Snow White's telephone began to ring and even though she rejected the call, he thought he spotted Gretchen's avatar image briefly popping up on the screen. It was unlikely that any other avatar would resemble hers: a reddish atomic mushroom with, as its stem, a rear view of her naked torso, in front of which was emblazoned a thick plait of braided hair fanning out expansively from the crown of the mushroom head.

Atam cautioned them that only calls that were vetted by him were to be made in his apartment given that everything was bugged. Snow White responded by sticking her tongue out at him, which made everyone laugh. In a conciliatory tone, Atam suggested that Fritz be locked in the bedroom but that he, Atam, should take the key with him so Fritz could not leave the apartment and he, Atam, would have free access to the bedroom on his return. He added that while the two women might want him to hand over the key, it was out of the question.

Snow White silently signalled her consent, but Bluebell interjected that such a solution would be utterly irresponsible if there was a fire, and so, they agreed that Atam would lock Fritz in the bedroom but that Bluebell would first fetch her bed linen from her room and leave it in his bedroom so that, in the event of an emergency, Fritz could abseil out of the room – but not simply walk out, at least not without some effort. Everyone agreed – except Fritz.

Feigning a fit of jealousy, Atam was eager to know why it had been alright for him to be locked up without any bed linen with which to escape and how he had been expected to save himself in the event of tremendous imminent danger. Snow White, eyelashes fluttering, said cryptically that every woman knew Atam was capable of anything. And in any case, they had only left him unattended for a short while. All they had wanted was to lock his firearm away in a safety deposit box at the Creditanstalt and do him a great favour in the process as he would soon realise.

XXIV

He ran down the stairs and slipped through the wine shop out onto the street without encountering anyone. Standing around smoking in front of the stage entrance to the Josefstadt Theatre were the usual workers in blue overalls. One of them was leaning casually against the door frame, one foot pressed up against the wall of the building. Atam glanced at him, shaking his head disapprovingly as he walked past, and the man hastily and rather sheepishly lowered his foot back down onto the asphalt.

At the Maria Treu, he eased himself onto a bar stool at the counter and signalled to the waiter, who immediately came over. He ordered a large glass of Muskateller – after all, together with Mimi and Fritz, he felt like one of the Three Musketeers – and four bottles to go, including three Grüner Veltliners and one Riesling from the Kamptal wine-growing region.

Sipping contentedly from the chilled dew-pearled glass, he turned around to look at the square, but apart from the plague column nothing caught his eye. In his mind he compared it with the Shila Devi temple in the forecourt of the three-thousand-year-old Amber Fort back home in Rajasthan, which looked like a giant wedding cake and had been built around the same time.

It was noon when he stepped out onto the pavement, and the bells of the basilica were ringing just as his stomach was rumbling. Atam briefly considered going back inside for a quick meal but felt it would be uncharitable to keep Fritz waiting, and so, he hurried home. He was amazed at how quickly circumstances had evolved and that there were now two women waiting for him in his apartment. He picked up his pace as he recalled that Mimi had also been to his apartment and that Andrea would probably turn up at his place very soon too. He prayed they would not all converge there at the same time.

Snow White opened the apartment door and this time she was smiling. He entered, carried the bottles into the kitchen and put them in the fridge – except for the Riesling, which he intended to open immediately. Bluebell walked into the kitchen. 'The key if you please,' she said. But he shook his head and instead placed a glass of wine in her outstretched hand. He carried the other glasses into the living room on a round silver tray.

'At last,' said Fritz once Atam had freed him from the bedroom. 'I was beginning to think you'd gone off somewhere for lunch.' He followed Atam into the living room where they all toasted one another's health. 'Cheers!' exclaimed Bluebell exuberantly. Fritz still had his glass raised to his lips as she walked up to him and began to fiddle with his belt in a bid to untie it. Ultimately, she found it too difficult to do so one-handed, so she held her glass out for Fritz to hold. Bluebell now deftly undid his belt with both hands, and as she pulled Fritz's light grey uniform trousers down over his hips, she squealed with delight. Fritz instantly downed Bluebell's glass of wine and then his own, his eyes staring wide the whole time. Standing there with his trousers around his ankles, he urgently called for more wine.

Atam fetched the half-empty Riesling bottle from the kitchen and topped up the glasses while Snow White picked up a small bright red package from the table and handed it to him. He opened it and took out an odd-looking rubber bundle. He located the green mouthpiece, put it to his lips and as he unfolded the polyvinyl chloride outer skin into a basin-shaped receptacle that dangled limply in his hands, he continued to blow air into it, softening its contours.

The paddling pool gradually acquired its definitive shape, even though its sides were not yet firm enough to hold water, and so, he stopped inflating it and held it out to Snow White. She pushed his arm away towards Bluebell, saying, 'It's her idea,' but Bluebell shook her head vigorously. 'No, it's a man's job,' she replied, and so, he finally handed it over to Fritz. It took a considerable effort on Fritz's part to finish the task, given that he was forced to fend off repeated and sustained attacks from Bluebell while he had his trousers down. He dodged her assaults, alternately turning away or holding the wobbly rubber item in front of him like a shield or using it to push Bluebell aside. She would repeatedly knock it out of his hands, which meant he had to start inflating it all over again several times. During these short breathers, Atam offered him some more wine, this time a Grüner Veltliner as the Riesling was finished.

At long last, Fritz was satisfied with the firmness of the paddling pool and set it down at his feet. As he stepped out of his lowered uniform trousers, Bluebell promptly whisked them away and dashed about the living room, swinging her vestimentary spoils above her head like a trophy and whooping triumphantly. She then disappeared into her room with it, only to reappear moments later with another folded paddling pool – an orange one this time – and held it out to Fritz: 'Do it. For my sake.'

Fritz unfolded the item and immediately found the ultramarine mouthpiece. Buoyed by the momentum of his previous success, he began to inflate the mini-paddling pool almost to its full size. Once again, he had to fend off Bluebell's continual attacks and assaults. He then tried to hand it over to Bluebell to keep her occupied and not leave her hands free to pull down his underpants. Bluebell, however, pushed his outstretched arm holding the almost inflated paddling pool towards Atam, who now willingly took hold of it. After all, it was only fair that he should take over from Fritz this time, just as Fritz had come to Atam's rescue earlier on.

Atam stood in front of the window for some fresh air and carried on inflating the paddling pool as fast as he could. All of a sudden, Snow White leaned over towards Atam and, with a deft and nimble grip, undid his belt and pulled his trousers down to his ankles. Atam instantly stopped what he was doing and almost let all the air out again. 'Do that and you'll never see your gun again; plus, you'll never find out what you've been chosen to do for us,' she said.

Already rather tipsy, he fought back the urge to get angry. But his curiosity regarding his mysterious assignment soon got the better of him, not to mention his desire to try his luck with Snow White. He even willingly stepped out of his trousers, which were again whisked away by Bluebell, not Snow White. Atam placed the paddling pool in front of the window and then rewarded himself with a large gulp of wine from his glass, staring wide-eyed the whole time.

Snow White decided it was time to fill the paddling pools. Chuckling, Atam and Fritz followed her instructions. Entranced as they already were by the dream-like scenario of this little orgy, they failed to realise just how awkward it was to carry the two hectolitres of water needed to fill the two pools from the kitchen to the living room using nothing other than empty milk bottles. As if in some pain, Snow White began to purse her lips at the unsatisfactory progress they were making. 'It's going to have to go a lot faster than this,' she remarked. 'How else are we supposed to manage it during the twenty-minute interval at the opera house?'

Atam squinted, pointing out that it would be better if everyone at the opera were to inflate their own paddling pools at the same time. It was about choreographing the synchronicity within the group. Snow White laughed warmly at his wonderful suggestion, blinking with both eyes. Atam, emboldened by his success, went on to say that everyone should also undress at the same time and then begin to fill up their pools, with everything once again performed in sync. At this suggestion she blinked so intensely that it looked like she had something in her eyes. With an amused smile, she asked Atam whether he would like to see her naked. She then hitched up her short dress and proceeded to dance around and perform a few steps of cancan in an endless repetitive loop but without kicking her legs upwards. The way Snow White merely raised her legs and angled her calves was so delightful that Atam was ready to do anything for her.

Meanwhile, Fritz was concerned that the paddling pools were far too low to be able to dive into and that, anyway, it would be impossible to smuggle in so much water unnoticed and get it past the ushers, enough in any case to be able to dive into the pools even if their sides were higher. 'Good old Fritz, you're so smart!' said Bluebell, spontaneously slapping his shoulder. Then, after a moment's hesitation, she added, 'We'll just have to drench ourselves from above!' And with that, she grabbed Fritz's hand and held it up against her cheek.

Atam reached out for Snow White's knee, but she leapt away teasingly, once again offering a glimpse of her vintage panties of unbleached cotton before tugging down the hem of her minidress and putting her index finger up to her lips just as Andrea had done to the Brigadier. From behind her index, she whispered that Atam had not seen anything yet and that, in a moment, she would put her fine stockings on for him, providing of course that he got down on his knees to implore her and vowed to do anything she wanted.

And so, Atam got down on his knees, asked Snow White to make herself beautiful for him and vowed to do whatever she asked of him. She flashed him a victor's cold, hard smile and ordered him to undress while she went to her room to get ready. Atam stripped off completely and laid his clothes neatly on a chair. Snow White soon returned, wearing nothing other than black loden stockings held up by a broad green flaxen garter belt adorned with coloured rhinestones. And in her orthopaedic shoes with the copper spiral springs that clacked twice with every step, she walked straight towards Atam.

She hummed a Gregorian melody after Hildegard von Bingen as she did so, clapping in time with the clacking of her footwear. Time and again she halted and wiggled her head sideways or moved it back and forth as one might in an Indian dance. Bluebell hummed the second voice and mimicked Snow White's every move. As the siblings converged in the middle of the room, they lined up side by side and let the singing and clapping fade away, stamping their feet until the very last note.

XXV

Fritz drove Atam to the Creditanstalt in the army limousine and, as a precautionary measure, pulled up at the bus stop on the other side of the street, opposite the main entrance. Atam marched straight into the building via the foyer on Schottenbastei and descended the vast beige marbled staircase to the basement. He walked through the wide array of glass-panelled chrome swing doors blocking off the entire deserted corridor and entered the large low-ceilinged hall with its U-shaped arrangement of safe deposit boxes. By then, it was already quite late and dusk had fallen, with little in the way of daylight filtering in from above through the translucent ceiling. He had met no one along the way inside the Creditanstalt and was alone in this hall too. He walked along the metal lockers and glanced at the key fob to check the locker number. 'No. 333' proved to be a walk-in safe. He quickly unlocked it and, resolute, stepped inside. He made himself reasonably comfortable on the rolled-up field-grey army blanket before pulling the door shut behind him. Snow White had left a large attaché case behind, the contents of which he now began to peruse. In addition to a chunky torch, he found a mini-safe with a timer that would only open at dawn to release the key to the locker, with his firearm, a bar of chocolate and the book *Zen and the Art of Surviving Inside an Egyptian Burial Chamber*. It had a handwritten dedication made out to Atam. Instead of dotting the 'i', she had drawn a little heart, and the book itself was written by her grandfather, an eminent authority on Egyptology at the LSA at Michigan State University.

There was an overwhelmingly pungent fragrance – that of Harmstaedter's pointedly masculine aftershave. There was also something hard pressing up through the blanket that turned out to be Harmstaedter's thermos flask, identical in design to the one he had been given in a jute sack for his afternoon snack. Out of curiosity, he opened the flask: it smelled of black tea with curdled milk, with an added dash of cognac. Nothing was left of Harmstaedter's provisions.

After reading the introduction and the first chapter by the light of the torch, Atam felt his stomach rumbling, and so, he cautiously opened the locker door and peeked out. It was dark, with only the red standby lights of the fire alarm sensors twinkling magically on the ceiling. He stepped out and walked around to stretch his legs. Then he spread the blanket out on the marble floor and settled down to enjoy his snack. It proved unexpectedly decent of the two siblings to have packed him two bread rolls filled with cold cuts and pickles, given that they themselves only ate vegan. Afterwards, he stretched himself right out on the blanket, wrapping his feet in a corner of the woollen plaid as his feet had quickly got cold. Slowly but surely, he drifted off to sleep, thanks to a relaxation technique he had had a habit of using while on various missions.

A few hours later, his telephone rattled, signalling a message from Gretchen. She had grown tired of Kosteletzky and had ordered him to fetch Harmstaedter's photos so he would have a reason to leave her apartment without her having to blatantly kick him out. She asked Atam to hand the photos over to him only the following morning; otherwise Kosteletzky would be back at her apartment far too soon.

Suddenly, there was a clacking sound from inside the briefcase: evidently, the timer had unlocked the mini-safe. He took out the key complete with fob and was at last able to seek out the corresponding safe deposit box. It was of medium size and, besides his Browning, contained a full magazine, a silencer and a printed but unsigned order of the day instructing him to fetch more photos from another deposit box and hand them all over to Kosteletzky. He sniffed the paper and recognised Snow White's distinctive shea butter hand-cream. The silencer displeased him greatly. The fact notwithstanding that the original barrel of his Browning had had no thread whatsoever to screw the silencer into; the modern suppressor made of matt black titanium would be visually very obtrusive. Neither the material nor its appearance matched the elegance of his nickel-plated firearm. He pulled back the slide and also noticed that the new barrel was made of a lighter steel. He let the slide glide back into place and saw that the thread of the new barrel protruded somewhat, something he had not noticed at first glance, even though he had sensed that something was different.

Again, he felt he ought to listen to his gut instincts more. On that point, it also occurred to him that Snow White must have known that there were no standard issue silencers for the vintage firearms he favoured; otherwise, she would not have been able to obtain and retrofit a replacement barrel in the short time his Browning had been in her possession, overnight as it were. So, who was Snow White? What did she want from him? And how did she know he had been present at Harmstaedter's death?

He wondered whether Gretchen and Snow White knew each other, what Andrea's role was in the whole scenario, and why on earth was a second-rate Brigadier called for. The photographs could also be in a smaller safe deposit box. All the small safes were housed in the southern corner, and the beige lacquer on most of them was heavily scratched. Some of the locks even bore the traces of attempts at forced entry. One door panel, however, had a small deep circular dent next to the rosette of the lock. Something metallic was stuck inside it.

Running his fingers over the magazine in his jacket pocket somewhat absentmindedly, it occurred to him that Snow White had also replaced the cartridges. He pulled out the magazine and, instead of his own supersonic ammunition, found slower-loading rounds inside it. Snow White had thought of everything – except that he would never be stupid enough to try and shoot open a safe. In fact, Harmstaedter had been extremely lucky not to have put an end to his days himself while shooting open the safe. In a way, Harmstaedter should not have been able to shoot the safe doors open for him at all. So, either Harmstaedter's mission had been set up to fail because of Harmstaedter himself, or the planning was far more perfidious and impenetrable than he could grasp at that very moment. Either way, the situation was unsatisfactory.

And he was particularly irritated by the fact that his original barrel was gone.

Striking the bullet-impacted door panel of the deposit box with the palm of his hand, he found that it recoiled and then popped open. 'Well now,' he whispered to himself. He examined the inside of the box and found more photographs of trees and park benches. Of course, none of it had anything to do with Gretchen's ex-husband nor had Harmstaedter and Gretchen probably ever been married. However, he did not put it past Gretchen to string someone like Harmstaedter along for a while, the same way she was now stringing Kosteletzky along. He put the new photos into his jacket pocket with the others, pressed the door panel shut until it locked into place, and retreated back inside his own locker.

This time he got as far as the fifth chapter, which described in meticulous detail the unsuccessful attempts of archaeologists to survive tomb-raider booby traps, complete with forensic reports of the most common causes of death. It was then that he heard footsteps in the corridor. It was now seven in the morning and the bank was about to open. He perceived the sort of clanking sound a bunch of keys might make. They must be opening up, thought Atam. The footsteps receded, soon to be replaced by new and different footsteps coming closer. He heard his name being called and went to open the door, but it would not open. Kosteletzky knocked from the outside. 'Come in!' replied Atam. 'How amusing,' was the response. But still the door would not open. 'Oh just shoot the lock,' suggested Kosteletzky. Clearly, Kosteletzky was Harmstaedter's equal when it came to deficient intellects, although even Harmstaedter would not have suggested such a course of action. Atam rolled over onto his back and braced both his feet up against the metal door, pushing with all his strength; the door bent and creaked, but still it would not spring open. He then pounded the door with his heels until it finally gave way, and he rolled out.

He handed Kosteletzky all the photographs, packed his things into the attaché case and then put his arm through Kosteletzky's in an overly familiar way as he guided him out of the bank. At Schottenring, he put Kosteletzky on a tram heading out to the district of Währing, where Gretchen lived on the penthouse floor of a villa in the Cottage quarter, overlooking Arthur Schnitzler's Garden; he then hailed a taxi to take him back to his apartment. Sitting alone on the back seat, he found himself, somewhat paradoxically, missing Andrea. Even though she had never meant anything to him personally, the closeness they had feigned and simulated was like the memory of a beautiful and never-ending dream. By the same token, it occurred to him that she used the very stuff that dreams were made of for her manipulative ways, and he was instantly glad that he had been left unscathed by her and not been drawn into any new escapades. His thoughts drifted to Mimi. He thought of how wonderfully she had saved him that previous morning, that in spite of her erotomanic appearance – her augmented breasts and her overinflated lips – she was the most honest and modest woman of all, for she wanted nothing from him beyond the gratification of her simple-minded vanity.

Gathered in front of his building was a contingent of police officers and ambulance-men greater than the available parking spaces could accommodate, and so, he asked the driver to drop him off further on at the traffic lights. Slowly, he strolled past the wine shop on the opposite pavement and counted five emergency vehicles with rotating blue lights. The crews were standing out on the pavement, staring into the wine shop, unsure as to how to proceed. Deciding not to tempt fate, Atam opted instead to steer a course towards the Maria Treu coffeehouse and treat himself to a decent breakfast.

XXVI

Having fortified himself, Atam strolled into Schönborn Park and settled on a bench in the shade at the foot of the bunker. He wrote a number of notes to Snow White and Fritz. Then he stretched right out and, with his head resting on his briefcase, fell fast asleep. He must have been asleep on the bench for quite a while by the time he was woken by the sound of kids shouting and screaming. They were yelling from all sides, and he could hear a ball bouncing off the bunker. Atam stood up and, with his briefcase tucked under his arm, withdrew behind a bush to relieve himself.

It was then that the ball rolled towards him into the elder bush, and he could hear the clatter of children's feet as they hurried over. He hastily adjusted his attire and kicked the ball back out onto the path. A girl wearing a helmet stopped the ball with her foot. Rather than thank him, she began to shout at him, asking what sort of peasant he was and wasn't he ashamed of himself. After all, only children were allowed to do what he was doing, and adults should use the public WC. What's more, he hadn't even washed his hands. Atam apologised and walked over to the fountain to do as he was told. Now he saw a whole group of children approaching. He noticed that their faces bore the expression of tremendous and utterly misplaced determination. They all wore helmets, trainers on their feet and colourful and oversized uniformly different T-shirts flapped around their bodies; each sported its own slogan printed in English: 'Earth First' and 'Stop the Change', for instance. Written across the girl's chest were the words 'Baby Today Carbon Tomorrow'. They were all holding large phones.

Evidently, some of them were phoning each other while others were engrossed in their screens as they came forward, without slowing down or stumbling. Others still performed risky manoeuvres on their electric scooters that whirred loudly whenever they accelerated. The kids wore earbuds connected to their phones by flimsy wires and spoke incessantly as if they never ever paused to listen. The girl had long-flowing auburn hair that spilled out from under her helmet. A metal guard was affixed in front of her face. Suddenly, she pointed at Atam and in an instant, he was surrounded by her entire entourage, the circle closing in ever tighter. Then she stretched her arms out in front of her and drew them apart horizontally, forming a semicircle. Abruptly, the children came to a standstill and held their ground. The girl signalled to a boy and pointed her index finger at Atam. The boy immediately held his large phone up towards Atam and then nodded to his leader.

'This is our park,' the girl said to Atam. 'What are you doing here anyway?' Atam rubbed his eyes and stared at the children surrounding him in an uneven circle. 'I'm on the run,' he confessed, which was not entirely untrue. He thought that perhaps the children might take pity on a fugitive. 'What have you done?' the girl wanted to know as she positioned herself closer to Atam as if to signal, he was being cornered. Atam replied that the police had pulled up outside his home. 'Are you a murderer?' asked the girl threateningly and with extreme anger. 'No, no!' said Atam to the girl beseechingly and began to walk away. But he had barely taken a step when another child shouted that the man was a motorist, that he'd seen him at the wheel of a car.

Then all hell broke loose. The girl reached into her jacket pocket and took out a chain, which she started swinging around furiously above her head, shouting 'Get him!' to her troops. All the children who previously had surrounded him suddenly pounced on him as one, dragging him down to the ground, kicking him, pulling his hair and punching him in the ribs. As he lay prone on the ground clutching his briefcase, they jumped onto his chest and stomach and squatted down on his legs. With his patience finally at an end, he grabbed the children one by one, pulling them off him and casting them aside until the girl with the chain took aim at his face. Atam kicked out at the girl, who fell backwards her full length and started to cry. Then, out of nowhere, he felt a hand slap him hard on the face from behind and heard Mimi's sharp voice chiding him for beating up little girls too.

At that point the girl, who was now back on her feet, asked Mimi if she was their new leader. Mimi nodded and pulled the girl closer to her, removing her helmet and straightening her tousled hair as she spoke to them all: 'This man belongs to me and you need to protect him and keep him out of harm's way.' The children nodded and stared at Atam as if to memorise his features, then back at Mimi. Suddenly, police sirens could be heard approaching at high speed up Florianigasse while other police cars drove up Alserstrasse towards Lange Gasse.

The children scattered and made a dash for the exit on Florianigasse, but already a handful of police officers were coming towards them from that very direction, wearing helmets and brandishing transparent shields in front of their faces. The children instantly turned on their heels and streamed towards the exit on Lange Gasse, the one Atam and Mimi were also aiming for just as a police van with flashing blue lights and wailing sirens pulled up in front of them. The doors flew open and a flow of police officers cascaded out onto the pavement and surged into the park.

Atam, Mimi, and the children veered away and leapt into the bushes, clambering over the low wire-mesh fence to the dog enclosure and running as fast as they could to the corner of Florianigasse and Lange Gasse. Behind them they could hear a policewoman shouting excitedly through a megaphone, ordering everyone to get down on the ground immediately and lie face down with their arms and legs spread out or they would be forced to make use of their firearms; indeed, warning shots could already be heard.

'Come on!' Mimi and the girl yelled, and the children ran hell for leather over towards the historicist-style fence that separated the park grounds from the pavement. Atam and Mimi gave each of the children in turn a leg-up, catapulting them over the fence. Atam then helped Mimi over. By then, the police officers had surrounded the bushes and were drawing their cordon ever tighter. Mimi stamped her plimsolls impatiently on the asphalt as Atam nimbly negotiated the fence and promptly landed at Mimi's feet. 'Nice going,' she cooed.

As they walked back along Lange Gasse into Maria-Treu-Gasse, Mimi remarked that she felt well past the age for that sort of early morning exercise before work, especially as she would now be standing around the shop all day, running back and forth attending to exemplary yet overwhelmed mothers with their ill-bred, coughing and spluttering children, snotty-nosed brats in any case, as they searched high and low for some even more divine and virtually extinct type of cereal grain cultivated in South America by an indigenous tribe with their bare hands under a full moon. Complimenting Mimi on her appearance, Atam enquired as to why she ran an organic health food store in the first place if it got on her nerves so much. Mimi giggled and replied that she would much prefer to be working in the fashion industry. She dreamt of having her own small boutique that never opened before ten in the morning at the earliest and did not have an adjoining workshop as she herself could not sew and employees were expensive.

By now they had reached Mimi's shop on Laudongasse. She rummaged around her large bag for quite a while searching for the keys, which gave her ample opportunity to ask Atam whether he might cook for her that day. He was amazed at how pleasantly surprised he was by her question, genuinely so. However, he was unable to give her a definite answer as he had no idea what would come of Snow White's plot for him later on that day. He promised to do his best. Mimi believed him. All of a sudden, everything was so easy between them. She handed him her apartment key and said she would be delighted if he could manage it. Then she stood on tiptoe and briefly pressed her lips to his mouth. Still on tiptoe she said she would love to cook for him but was a hopeless cook. He believed her. She giggled bashfully and stepped back.

Atam was now convinced that he was in no danger from Mimi; in fact, in his mind, Mimi was beginning to turn into something of a little angel, one he had misjudged because of its disguise and of whom he had proved himself unworthy for taking her literally. But he did not have the time right then to deal with Mimi as he had to find out how things stood with Snow White and Gretchen, and so, he called Kosteletzky. 'You know you're not supposed to call me,' he began, 'seeing that we're being tapped?' 'My phone is tap-proof,' Atam replied, 'and no one is interested in you yet.' 'Are you with Gretchen?' 'Yes, we've now got everything together, thanks. But you are not to call her for the next few days. She'll be in touch.' 'Who is Snow White anyway?' 'A fairy-tale character created by the Brothers Grimm,' and with that he rang off. Atam began to wonder what the photographs could be about. The depictions themselves were unimportant; of that he was convinced. Perhaps the photographs would have to be subjected to graphical analysis to get to the information. Or perhaps some banned chemical substances were embedded in the gelatin of the photographs? Where had the photographs actually come from? And why would they be of any interest to a fairy-tale character in a flaxen garter belt? He felt a strange desire swelling up inside him.

XXVII

Atam thought he had better not ignore Snow White's instruction for the time being and to avoid his apartment; after all, who knew what other traps she had set up there, the police patrol notwithstanding! He did not under any circumstances want to go to Uncle László's for he had yet to draw her out and get her to break cover. Was she really just the pretty face of some petty women's association working for the salvation of the planet that drowned bad guys so there would be more room and more air for the good guys? Someone who had sacrificed Harmstedter as a pawn and wanted to use him as a sacrificial pawn too just as he would use Kosteletzky as a pawn? Was there a toxic self-annihilating order behind it all that wanted to eliminate humankind in order to protect Mother Earth? Was it all just a trick to get him out of circulation? If so, who might be the contracting party?

Having already dispatched single-handedly so many mortal enemies of his infallible order, he had acquired the sobriquet 'Archangel Michael'. But he had always been so cautious and so meticulous that there could not have been anyone left who wanted to come after him. Provided he did not get himself into trouble out of sheer wantonness or recklessness, nothing would happen to him – of that, he was sure. In fact, he felt almost untouchable. He felt that the most reasonable course of action was probably simply to assume that 'the world was everything that was the case'. And it was certainly the case that he was unarmed at that moment. He headed to Josefgasse to see his arms dealer, keen to look for an original gun barrel in the spare parts store of the adjoining workshop. As he entered the store, he was discreetly informed by the senior sales manager that a call had been received for him and that he was to inform the Herr Commander that Snow White was the stepmother. 'Are you absolutely sure?' 'I did not have the honour of speaking to the Governor in person, but my colleague wrote it down for me to tell you, and that is precisely what it says here on this note: Snow White is the stepmother.'

While Atam rummaged around for a barrel inside a wooden box of leftover bits of Browning Hi-Power, he was almost overwhelmed by a sense of tremendous surprise as to how the Governor might know he was with Snow White. It was not so much the fact that he might know but that he wanted to know. Of course, the Governor had the possibility at all times to know everything there was to know about his moves, but usually, and for the sake of simplicity, he would just have asked him, had he been that interested. 'Why was it any different now?' Atam wondered, and he had an inkling that Gretchen's association might not be that petty after all. Until now he had dismissed her inconsistencies and the bizarre succession of coldness and empathy, not to mention flaring hot temper, merely as the whims of a somewhat overindulged woman. But evidently, she played very different roles on different levels, occasionally tunnelling from one to the next simply because whatever she was up to would be so monstrous that she herself could not stand it. And so, she constantly had to flit over to a lighter role in order to recover and restore in herself a sense of normality. He had previously had an occasion to observe something similar in a number of assassins and managed to entice them towards one of their normal roles in order to neutralise them all the more easily. Indeed, nothing was more difficult to achieve than neutralising activists who were not quite themselves, at least not without inflicting major collateral damage.

He had by now found several barrels; lost in thought, he went down to the firing range to break them in. Unprompted, the shooting range officer loaded the same program as last time; it had been stored under his name. And so, the unknown female spectator was once again in the landau carriage in the Prater meadows. Atam requested a target, and a wooden pole with a shooting target was played into the meadow scenery. Of the three barrels, one was useless, but the other two were true in their point of impact and barely strayed. As the target dissolved, the DUELL program continued to run. All of a sudden, the characters began to jump around and instead of the mystery woman, an unflattering photograph of Harmstedter was superimposed as the observer, somewhat incongruous in the landau carriage; Snow White stepped into the ring as the faceless adversary. Without waiting for the random generator, she took aim at Atam and fired three times in quick succession. While the first bullet missed Atam completely or struck him elsewhere than the electric vest, the second impacted as a shot through the lungs with sickening pain. Someone on the outside must have hacked into the program, not just replacing the protagonists but also setting the amperage to an unacceptably high level, one that should not even be available. The third shot hit dead air as Atam ripped the cable out of the console after the second shot and fired a bullet through Snow White's forehead.

As he had neither sought out his apartment nor gone to Uncle László's to flush out Snow White, he did not think he would run into her in the shooting gallery of all places, and certainly not in this way. He had the feeling this appearance would corroborate the Governor's message, but he was not convinced as to who had formulated it. Was it a coincidence, then, that Snow White, as an effigy, should want to shoot him – rather unsportingly – at this very moment, contrary to all the rules? Or was it meant to be a signature move on the Governor's part, designed to cut short any further considerations and underscore the urgency of the task? Atam was, at any rate, prepared for anything.

On no account, he thought, should he now go back to what was supposed to be his apartment. Snow White may well have disposed of Bluebell there in order that he might be withdrawn from circulation by the police as a murderer once he had fulfilled his mission with the photos. Certainly, Bluebell had never been Snow White's half-sister. They looked far too dissimilar for that to be the case. Bluebell had probably been a naïve captive of the Environmental Protection Society or a pawn that was no longer needed since the photos had already reached Gretchen. The difference in social standing between the two women had been far too great, and it appears that Snow White had granted Bluebell the right to play along merely in order to humour her. He could go to Andrea's apartment if the apartment on Alserstrasse was indeed her apartment at all, something he could readily ascertain with a minor break-in; alternatively, he could go into hiding at Mimi's. If so, he ought to cook her something and that would entail going shopping first; after all, he did not want to have to make do once again with the mould-ridden supplies from her kitchen.

XXVIII

Just as Atam was considering breaking into Andrea's apartment, as if by telepathy of some kind, his phone rang, with Andrea on the line. Purringly, she explained that she had been unable to bear the thought of being without her darling Atam any longer and that, thanks to oodles of feminine guile, she had managed to persuade the Brigadier to organise a car for her so she could return to the family fold. She had fought like a lioness to get transferred to the Rossau Barracks as a secretary so that in future, she could walk to her office, which would be no further away than her previous place of employment on Ringstrasse. Although eager to know where Atam was, Andrea did not give him a chance to answer, preferring instead to continue chatting. She explained she was currently sitting in the back of a green limousine belonging to the 6th Mountain Infantry Brigade and was about to turn into Alserstrasse. Laughing merrily, Andrea added that this time, she did have the right keys in her hand. Atam replied that he was about to come anyway, but before he could elaborate further, she oohed and aahed lasciviously, giggled and then abruptly hung up.

Presumably, Andrea was now planning to eliminate him in the stairwell, either herself or through the Brigadier's intercession; after all, who knows what terrible things she must have told him about Atam. Breaking into her apartment was now superfluous; indeed, the fact that she had summoned him there was tantamount to an admission that she did not reside there at all and that the keys would never have fitted that particular lock. He wondered how far this succession of recruitments and executions would go and what good this escalation would do. There would always be someone left who would, in turn, have to be eliminated by the next newcomer – unless of course one could depend on finding losers such as Harmstedter, who could be relied upon to eliminate themselves. Or someone like the Brigadier, Mr Loyal-to-one-woman-for-life, who was naive enough to believe whatever the likes of Andrea might tell him, even though he himself was leading her by the nose.

But Atam's main concern now was for Fritz. As he still had not heard back from him, Atam had to assume that Fritz had been eliminated by Snow White or perhaps even eliminated first before Snow White killed Bluebell. Atam headed towards the Astoria Garage on Trautsongasse to fetch his car. He took the lift to make sure he would not be out of breath from running up the stairs and that his hands would not be shaky as a result. Before walking over to his car, he halted and listened. Then, pretending to get into the adjacent car, he threw himself to the ground and rolled over towards his own car. He lay there, waiting and listening. Still recumbent, he unlocked the car door and slid silently into the driver's seat. With tyres humming, he drove down the spiralling ramp to the ground floor. Upon reaching Zeltgasse, he slowed down and noticed that there were still police cars parked in front of the wine shop.

He instructed the voice-assisted AI on his phone to call Snow White, but she did not pick up, nor did her answering service activate; instead, her phone disconnected after five rings. He then told his phone to dial Gretchen's number. She answered and, rather breathlessly, explained that she was on her way to a demo on the Hernalser Gürtel orbital and asked Atam to meet her beneath the suburban railway arch of the Alserstrasse station in fifteen minutes. She told him she had something for him and then hung up. Atam switched on the car radio and searched for a local news station. There were apparently two demos. One along the inner Hernalser Gürtel, 'For Good', and one along the outer Hernalser Gürtel, 'Against Evil'. How annoying, he thought, that he had no idea what side Gretchen would be on. At the traffic lights at Otto-Mathias-Hauer Platz along Josefstädterstrasse, he discreetly slid a full magazine into his Browning, pulled the slide right back and then released it sharply to load the chamber, secured it with the hammer half-cocked, and then tucked the gun into his vintage leather shoulder holster beneath his jacket. He was determined to save Fritz.

On Breitenfelder Gasse, there was no way of getting across the orbital road, so heavily attended was the 'For Good' demo. Already from Albertplatz he could see the floats and crowds of people densely packed together, standing around trance-like. The noise of firecrackers and drums punctuated by slogans chanted from huge loudspeakers reached right inside the car, drowning out the radio reporter trying to explain those very slogans. At the corner of Blindengasse, the police were diverting all the traffic, but Atam flashed his ID and stated that he was there to pick someone up from the police station and was allowed through. He parked right next to the entrance to the Federal Immigration Office and let himself be carried along by the 'For Good' procession on the inner orbital in the direction of Alserstrasse.

It was then that he received a text message from Gretchen telling him to enter the Alserstrasse station and meet her up on the Westbahnhof-bound platform. Atam hurried downhill and, shortly thereafter, entered the station. As he hurried up the stairs, he noticed that the station was deserted. It was only when he stepped out onto the platform that he spotted three women at the very end of the canopied platform: Snow White and Gretchen, with Mimi between them. Mimi looked distraught and as he got closer, he noticed that she was in fact being propped up and was sobbing, her head lolling back and forth. As she spotted him, she screamed at him to run away, promptly eliciting a punch in the face from Gretchen that burst her nose open, causing it to bleed profusely. Gretchen yelled at Atam, saying they would throw Mimi under the next train if he didn't toe the line.

From below he could hear cheerful music blaring and PA-distorted announcements similar to those in Neudeggergasse two days previously, only much, much louder. So even without the silencer, the two shots he fired would never have been heard. Gretchen and Snow White instantly collapsed onto the platform. Mimi dropped to her knees, bracing herself with her hands to prevent her face from striking the ground. She shrieked as she suddenly spotted the two small bullet holes in the women's foreheads and tried to scramble to her feet. Atam helped her up and brushed the hair away from her face. Half crying and half laughing, she asked where he had learnt his manners, frightening her like that. He in turn enquired as to Fritz's whereabouts. Fighting off the tears that were causing her mascara to run, she replied that he had gone to ground in Tyrol, but with his mountain infantry unit, not his grandparents, as he was worried the two women might track him down. Atam sat Mimi down on a bench and then went over to drag Snow White and Gretchen away from the platform edge and off to one side, leaning them upright against each other so their bullet holes would not be immediately apparent. He returned to Mimi, who was trying to patch the holes at the knees in her laddered tights with the blood from her nose. He jokingly asked whether she too had just come down off the hills, prompting Mimi to chuckle. He promised that he would cook for her later on that day.

XXIX

Mimi clung to his side and managed to keep pace with him, albeit limping slightly. They marched along with the procession on the outer, suburban side of the orbital road to get back quickly to his car on the city centre side. The barricades erected under the Breitenfelder archway meant that they were forced to continue marching to the station at Josefstädter Strasse. After walking through the building, they joined the procession moving in the opposite direction on the inner ring-road and reached the police station on Breitenfelder Gasse without any further incident.

Atam opened the passenger door so Mimi could get in. She slipped into the seat bottom-first, looking back down the street as she did so. It was then that she noticed an electric car accelerating silently, heading straight for her. She tried to leap out and escape, but stumbled in her high heels and fell to the ground. She called out Atam's name, with the unexpected new-found familiarity she had always longed for and now enjoyed with this man, knowing with certainty that he would save her and that only he would ever have been in a position to do so. Already Atam had trained his firearm on the driver of the car. The cartridge cases from half the magazine arced over the roof of his car in a rapid fire and tinkled down onto the asphalt. The white electric car, its tyres shot to ribbons, skidded and swerved into the parked vehicles and came to a stop with a loud crashing and screeching. Andrea's forehead now sported a small bullet hole and her head lurched forward onto the steering wheel, triggering the horn, which then blared continuously. The car driving up behind Andrea failed to stop in time and, with its tyres squealing, careered into the back of her vehicle, causing its boot to pop open and disgorge Fritz's body, his arms and legs bound with dark grey duct tape. Such was the force of the impact that it catapulted two gas cylinders affixed with large skull-and-bones stickers up into the air. After a haunting moment of gravity-defying flight, they twirled their way above Fritz, then clattered to the ground, striking the asphalt hard and snapping off their screw caps. A highly pressurised gas began to hiss out, painting a pink vapour trail into the air.

Then, behind Atam, just a few yards off to the side, a single gunshot was fired. He felt something searingly hot on his chest and instinctively reached up to a spot where his shirt was now wet and sticky. He felt as messy and as soiled as he had back then when he had finally acquiesced to inviting the governor to his grandmother's house after the latter had pleaded with him for years beforehand. Overawed by the occasion, the governor had mislaid his spectacles while prostrating himself for the reverential salutation, prompting him, in all the excitement, to place his hand on the wrong foot. Quickly and unobtrusively, Atam had pulled him away by his left foot in order to shift the focus of this uncanny moment onto himself;

he was, after all, naturally well-versed in dealing with such situations. Now he was intent on wiping away this soiling, but the source of this warm sticky substance oozing from his person somehow seemed plentiful. Feeling a painless yet sharp stinging in his body, it slowly began to dawn on him that he might have been struck by a bullet. Was this the merciless, delayed result of the wrong *pranama* salutation? What did he know? Everything was surreal. He turned around slowly and saw everything unfolding in staggered slow motion. A policeman was striding towards him, eyes wide open with fear in a face distorted by yelling. In his unsteady hands, he held a plastic firearm well out in front of him and was gesturing wildly with it. His legs sagged slightly at the knees with every step, causing the kit dangling from his belt to swing and jingle in time, like a merry-go-round.

Atam tried to stay upright; clutching shut the wound in his chest. With every heartbeat and breath, foaming blood commingled with specks of lung tissue and bright splinters of bone oozed from between his fingers. He found most upsetting the fact that he sensed no pain. Despite the broken ribs and the blood loss, he felt nothing. He feared he was in hypovolemic shock, and a faintness appeared to be descending upon him, one from which he was afraid he might never escape. He despised the pathetic figure of the policeman as a helpmate to all that was disturbing and hostile, made as ever of the sturdiest stuff and logically evolved from an axiomatic foundation. It was all so ridiculously irritating. From the nature of his wound, he realised that the policeman had used hollow point ammunition rather than a full metal jacket bullet, and he felt an indignant rage surge within him. There could be no doubt that he had been destined for greatness, for he had always sensed tremendous forces within him. Was he now to meet a senseless end at the hands of some clumsy oaf? In his mind, his entire past and the whole history of his royal lineage in Rajasthan flashed before his eyes and despite himself, he wondered what he had lived for. To what end had he been born? Had he not been an enlightened soul in this world, as his name evoked? And what had he achieved and, indeed, given to the world?

The policeman was now standing just a few feet in front of him, grimacing hysterically. His cheap uniform was made of synthetic fibres flecked with cheap cotton, his unflattering and creaseless cargo trousers stopped well short of his ankles to reveal bog-standard pale grey socks: in terms of ridiculous appearances, it was all so pathetic. Not to mention the hysterically distraught facial expression. How could Atam even contemplate being obliterated by such an insignificant and lowly minion? How could he entrust His Highness to the mere bureaucratic care of a subprime municipal hospital? He who himself had been master and commander over life and death? He raised the Browning to his head, placed the barrel against his temple, and pulled the trigger.

Mimi scrambled to her feet and lunged at the policeman. She threw him to the ground and began kicking him with her injured leg until she was overwhelmed by several officers rushing to the scene. She knocked two more policemen unconscious while a third, screaming in pain, rolled from the pavement onto the street and under Atam's car to take cover. With more and more police officers spilling out of the building, she eventually played dead and surrendered to her fate, handcuffed and shackled. When an ambulance finally drew up, Mimi inched over towards Atam to press herself up against him, rolling back and forth in his blood, head-to-head, her blond hair now unkempt. Around her eyes, her mascara and eye shadow blended into a dark grey wispy outline framing her cheeks reddened by the blood from her nose that matched the red garlands of blood on Atam's forehead, its majestic brown now glowing against the tarmac. Far away, on the Gürtel orbital road, loudspeakers on a passing float were blaring out Yoko Ono and John Lennon's Imagine.

By the time more ambulances arrived on the scene with their blues and twos, all the passers-by were lying scattered about the pavements, their bodies cramping in bizarre contortions, their unseeing eyes wide open and staring, and their teeth bared. The woman who had crashed into the back of Andrea's electric car had collapsed the instant she got out. Clearly, her demise was not due to shock or injury, for she too was lying next to her vehicle with a ghostly grin on her face and grotesquely twisted limbs. As they alighted from their vehicles, the paramedics too began to stagger among the dead and the dying until one after the other they went down in wild convulsions and lay prone with eerie grins and wide-open eyes staring fixedly.

Mimi appeared to be the only one unaffected by any of this. Breathing steadily, she got up into a crouching position, then closed Atam's eyes, tenderly stroking his face for the first time. She observed that everyone except for Atam and herself had been slain by this strange death. The distant music from the PA van fell silent and an eerie stillness spread, with only the loud chirping of the birds in the nearby park, the horn of

Andrea's car, the two-tone sirens of the ambulances, and the purring engines audible.

Mimi realised that it was only thanks to Atam's proximity that she had been spared the sinister extinction that had suddenly befallen everyone else. She took deep breaths in and out. Suddenly recalling her yoga in line with Atam's Indian ancestry, she practised her *ujjayi* breathing and was buoyed by her apposite association. She breathed out and then back in again, and still nothing bad happened to her. She was alive and felt a desperate lust for life. It occurred to her in a flash that with Atam, she could beget a new human race, one that would be immune to all evil and always do the right thing – just as she herself always did everything right because she listened to her deepest feelings, something she never got tired of mentioning.

She tried to work out where she was in her fertility cycle and had to resort to a number of mnemonic techniques to calculate when her last period had begun. She had, after all, been unprepared for such a situation and anyway, she never made notes of her cycle in her diary. She wondered how she might be able to get hold of Atam's semen. Desperate situations called for desperate measures, and nothing less than the survival of humanity was now at stake. Then again, she was hopeful she may have been at one with him during their nights together, which she barely remembered as she had had too much to drink; and anyway, those nights were now already part of another era. It struck her that she had been told on numerous occasions (the morning after, as it were) that she had at some point woken up in the middle of the night completely drunk and had befallen her male partner like a woman possessed. An avalanche of euphoria swept over her at this thought. However, such accounts had always been related to her with a cheerful twinkle of the eye, and she had no way of knowing how truthful they were. And then of course there was the Virgin Mary's immaculate conception. She remembered that once she had read something about it at school.